The Bloody Affray at Riverside Drive

The courts here in Chicago say I done a murder, and the newspapers say the same, but I say different. I wouldn't want to go to my execution with a bad name like 'murderer' hanging round my neck, so I took steps to clear my reputation. Once you've read what I writ here, you'll appreciate that what happened weren't no hasty, thoughtless brawl between strangers, like you can get, but a long-standing difficulty between old friends that could only be settled in one way. I've put it all down, all about the various folks that got tangled in this affair: Seth Walsh, who was a likeable young rip and a truly outstanding liar; Mr Johnston, who had a fine natural talent for gunplay; Handsome Henry Plumer, who was the most outrageous sheriff I ever struck. The women, too, like wild Lily Farmer; and Belle, whose name can still bring back the pangs of love. Also Mr Quarles, that rich old blister who had a lot to do with the way things turned out, when you come to think about it, as I sure hope you will, and oblige

MISSOURI FYNN

by the same author

Fiction
THE LAST DAYS
THE KNIFEMAN
THE REAPERS
STAG BOY
THE BAREBONES
THE WORLD TURNED UPSIDE-DOWN

Non-Fiction
THE TRIBE AND ITS SUCCESSORS

THE BLOODY AFFRAY AT RIVERSIDE DRIVE

William Rayner

Collins
St James's Place London, 1972

William Collins Sons & Co Ltd
London · Glasgow · Sydney · Auckland
Toronto · Johannesburg

First published 1972
© William Rayner, 1972
ISBN 0 00 221089 4
Set in Monotype Bembo
Made and Printed in Great Britain by
William Collins Sons & Co Ltd Glasgow

For SIMON and VAL
and the summer of '71

First, take a look at the piece that follows. I'm going to copy it out from Tuesday's *Chicago Mirror*, and let me say from the start that I am the Noah 'Missouri' Fynn the editor's going on about. Here's what he says:

The Bloody Affray At Riverside Drive

Now that the trial of Noah 'Missouri' Fynn is over, we listen confidently for certain predictable voices to be raised in objection, and sure enough, we are not disappointed. These voices plead for an extenuation of the death sentence passed on Fynn, and equally predictably, they claim to speak in the name of humanity and civilized values. We think we speak in defence of the same values, but it is our opinion that the sentence passed on Fynn should be carried out.

It is urged by those who speak in Fynn's defence that he is a product of the Frontier and should be judged in those terms. But are the qualities displayed by Fynn those of the many sturdy pioneering families settling our Western regions? We hardly think so! By his own admission, Fynn is a rootless drifter, and his associates have been mainly of the same kind. Seth Walsh began as a friend of Fynn's and the two of them then fell in with the man referred to as Mr Johnston, to form an ominous trio. Enquire how it was they came to befriend Mr Johnston and the answer is illuminating: they sought him out from admiration, after watching him slay a man! Indeed, of the three men in question, two at least are self-confessed murderers. Are we really asked to believe this typical of our Western pioneers? Give a thought to their friendship with the infamous Henry Plumer, sheriff of Helena. Is this association typical? Can we really believe that Fynn is telling the truth in his testimony on this subject?

We come on to firmer ground when we examine the relationship between Fynn and Mr and Mrs Quarles. We in Chicago have reason to respect Mr Quarles. We know him as an astute and upright man of business, whose enterprise has enriched the city, and whose encouragement of the arts has also had its beneficent effect on our community. Before he settled amongst us, Mr Quarles lived for a time in Helena, and it was here that he and Mrs Quarles first encountered Fynn. They did their best to help this young man, giving him employment and encouraging him to lead a decent and regular life. Mrs Quarles, in particular, laboured in this cause. Nor did the Quarleses waver in their support of Fynn, even when he and Seth Walsh came close to receiving the same summary justice that was at length handed out to the notorious Sheriff Plumer by an infuriated populace. Indeed, it was after this event that Mr Quarles proposed a business partnership to Fynn which could have been the making of him, but Fynn chose to throw away this opportunity and return to his aimless, drifting life, alone this time, after his quarrel with Seth Walsh and the disappearance of Mr Johnston.

It might be thought that fate would have allowed Mr and Mrs Quarles to live in peace after their removal to Chicago, but it was not to be. Mrs Quarles's Christian compassion towards an orphan child was to bring Fynn back into their lives, with fatal consequences. If we ask whose was the responsibility for the bloody affray at Riverside Drive, there is only one answer possible, on the evidence that has been offered: the trouble was deliberately provoked by Fynn and the subsequent murder and wounding were of his doing. It was a barbarous act, a blow against all civilized standards, carried out as it was among a gathering including some of Chicago's most eminent citizens. These good people found themselves involved without warning

8

in a scene of carnage and violence of a kind such as now and then disfigures the lowest saloons of the Frontier. It was the brutal and outrageous response of a man from whom the Quarleses had a right to expect gratitude, not mayhem.

Lastly, we must ask whether the bearing of Fynn since his arrest has been such as to incline right-thinking men towards leniency on his behalf. The answer must surely be 'No'. He has shown scant respect for the law, and has never once expressed remorse for his deed. There is no doubt the man is a murderer. Very well, then! Let there be no weakening in our resolve. Let us serve notice by his fate on those brutal and lawless elements in our society that we will no longer tolerate their presence in our midst. It is right that Fynn should die, not only in the name of justice, but in defence of the fundamental values of our new American civilization.

Well, I ain't dead yet, my lawyer has filed an appeal, but if I'm still around, it ain't the fault of the Chicago newspapers, and the *Mirror* in particular. The trouble is, when these newspaper fellers and lawyers get to work on a thing, they make it sound all different. I tore the above piece out of the *Mirror*, and studied it, and brooded on it, and what I come up with was: I'll have to write about the way things really were, because if I don't, who will? I'm not much of a hand at ciphering, but I'm going to have to try. It's going to be a considerable sweat, but my mind is made up. I mean to tell my story, even if nobody gets to read it, and the way I figure it, my best bet might be to pick up points from what the feller in the *Mirror* wrote. That way I can use him to blaze my trail for me, which is help I'm surely going to need.

If anybody should happen on these papers, I'd be obliged if they'd read them through – a man likes to think his voice might be heard, even when he's pretty sure the opposite will be the case. Well, here goes. I reckon this is about the best place to make a start:

I

Enquire how it was they came to befriend Mr Johnston and the answer is illuminating: they sought him out from admiration, after watching him slay a man!

How me and Seth got friends with Mr Johnston

There was a saloon on the outskirts of Cheyenne. It was morning but the sun was hot and bright already, which was the reason why Seth and me called into that saloon – not that Seth ever needed a reason for drinking. There was a long bar with a mirror fixed on the back wall, and round the floor there was tables, in the usual style. We stood up to the bar and chatted, and Seth studied himself in the mirror. Seth always was a man for a mirror. Let him near a mirror and he would keep throwing it little glances on the sly, like he was trying to take himself by surprise. Also he would stroke his moustache every now and then, and give his reflection a nod and a smile, as if to say: 'You're doing all right, partner. You're a handsome dog.' That was true enough: Seth *was* a handsome dog. He had dark gleaming eyes and long side-burns and black hair curling in his neck. Seth was a favourite with the ladies, and he knew his powers right well in that direction.

There was the two of us, taking it easy, with Seth sneaking them little glances at himself, when all of a sudden he went mighty still and his head poked forward on his neck like a hound dog on a scent. He was staring into the mirror. Naturally, I looked there, too, and what I saw was Mr Johnston, sitting all alone at a table in the corner, though of course I didn't know him by name at that time. Mr Johnston was slumped there, brooding, with his chin propped on his hand, and I must say he did look a grim sort of customer, with his muzzle of a beard and them pale grey eyes of his that weren't looking at anything just then, but was boring through the wall of the saloon and maybe right through this world and into the next.

Mr Johnston was lost in a dream, which was unfortunate, because just at that moment there was a feller creeping up on him, a little hard-faced man with slitty eyes and a narrow mouth, and a hand on his gun-butt. The little feller had a wild, desperate air about him, as if he'd only just managed to screw himself up to do what he intended, which was shoot Mr Johnston in the back.

Of the two of us, Seth moved first. He spun round and stepped towards the little feller, and at the first stride his gun was out. 'Hold it!' says Seth.

The little feller jumped like he'd been stung. Interruptions was the last thing he was looking for. He turned his head, slow and cautious, to see who was doing the ordering, and when his eyes fell on Seth, he glared in a way that was both scared and nasty. As for Seth, he went glaring back in the same style, and it struck me these two might have crossed trails somewhere before.

'Here's a little rat was fixing to draw on you,' says Seth to Mr Johnston. 'I thought you'd like to know.'

Mr Johnston blinked and come back to himself and rose up from his chair, and when he was on his feet, he turned out to be a long thin man with a noticeable stoop at the shoulders. He weren't a young man, neither, but getting on for forty, I reckon. His shoulders was narrow and he had long spidery legs with no swell to speak of at the calf; straight-up-and-down legs, you might say, cased in boots like stovepipes. He got up neat and quick, but he took the gun out of his holster slow, like it was heavy and he could hardly abide the weight of it. Then he turned his pale grey eyes on the little feller, and it was a sure thing that *them* two had met somewhere before.

'You!' That was all Mr Johnston said, but he said it in such a rasping, hollow voice, and with that queer accent on the word, you couldn't help feeling scared. Next he cocked his gun, which didn't improve matters. Men round about noticed that a fuss had started, and the room went that quiet, you could have heard a pin fall. The little feller's lip dithered and then he started gabbling and crying out.

'Look at me,' says the little feller. 'I'm standing here, defenceless. You wouldn't shoot me down in cold blood. You wouldn't do that!'

'Wouldn't I?' says Mr Johnston.

'Don't you mean to give me no show? You can't plug a man with no show,' says the little feller. 'That'd be plain murder, and it ain't fair.'

Mr Johnston didn't make no answer, so the little feller started calling out to the onlookers, asking them to bear witness of how he was being treated, how he was being gunned down with no chance to go for his weapon, which was out-and-out butchery. Nobody else ventured a word. I looked across to see how Seth was taking it, and I saw he was smiling again. Seth did a deal of smiling, and as often as not you couldn't figure out just exactly what he was smiling about. It was like that now.

'Shut your head,' says Mr Johnston to the little feller. 'I'm going to give you your chance. Step outside.'

As he went out, driving the little feller in front of him on the end of his gun, Mr Johnston says to Seth: 'I'm obliged to you, Mister, and would be even more if you'd keep a cover on this gentleman for me. He's the slippery sort and won't fight fair unless he's driven to it.'

'A pleasure!' says Seth, and ranged after them, nursing his gun. I followed, and so did everybody else that was in the bar. They all came crowding out and stood at the sides, in safe places along the board-walks, under the awnings, or peeping out of doorways.

Mr Johnston set it up fair and square. He didn't take no advantage. He did it all straight as string, and I admired him for it. 'Walk,' he says to the little feller, 'and when you get to ten paces, turn and fire. Would you be kind enough to call the paces?' says Mr Johnston to Seth, 'and if he tries any tricks like turning short – plug him.'

Seth nodded. He was smiling again.

One look at the little feller's face told you plenty. He must have known what he was up against. It looked like he wished himself a thousand mile from Cheyenne, but there weren't no help for it now, all he could do was face it out. Well, he buckled to the job as best he could, and I guess he hoped that luck might run for him, like men do, even when they know they don't stand a chance of coming out on top. Men always hope, but in my experience, luck ain't hardly ever that kind to the underdog.

Things make a big impression on you when you're young,

and this fight did on me. I won't never forget it. Lord, but it fell awful still as they begun their walk! There was the street, and the crowd hardly breathing, and a white face or two peeping out from the windows, and no noise at all, save for a horse that didn't know why it had gone so quiet or had maybe got the sweat of fear in his nostrils and started nickering. There weren't a cloud in the sky, and the light was hard and glaring. I can recall how the sun flashed on Mr Johnston's belt-buckle with every step he took, and away in the distance the heat was drawing up the smoke and the hills was a-tremble. I can still see their boots treading in the dust, and hear Seth's voice, sounding lonely as he called the paces. It was a sight to knock the breath out of your body.

Seth got to ten and both men whirled round. It was the most amazing thing to see how Mr Johnston's weapon leapt into his hand. He got off a round like lightning, and the slug took the little feller in the chest, while he was still hauling his iron out of the holster. The little feller never did get that gun clear. The force of Mr Johnston's bullet sent him staggering back, his hat fell off and pitched in the dust, and everybody gave a general sigh. They could see it was all over with the little feller, but he didn't just fall down; he took a few steps first, weaving round like a drunk man, and then a rush of the reddest blood came to his mouth, and he retched on it, and down he went and lay still.

Nobody could say that hadn't been a fair show on Mr Johnston's part, but when I looked at the little feller lying there, he did look awful small and smashed about. He looked like he'd been tossed aside, with his yellow hair trailing in the dirt, his arms and legs thrown anyhow, and blood leaking from his mouth and going black in the dust. He looked like a shot bird when she's fallen from the air, and her wings are crumpled and her feathers dirtied, and the ruby drop stands at the end of her beak. It was a dreary sight, and yet I knew the little feller had deserved it, and that what he'd got had come to him in fair fight, which was more than he aimed to give Mr Johnston. But I always did feel sad to see a man rubbed out, and I guess Mr Johnston didn't feel much different, the way he stood there, looking dazed, and his face a blank. When he holstered his weapon, it was like the gun had got heavy again, and he could hardly bear its weight. I wondered what it was the little feller had held against him, to go creeping up on him like that.

'That was pretty fair shooting,' says Seth, and I could hear from his voice that he was taken aback by the sheer speed that Mr Johnston had showed, but then, so was everybody. Naturally, he wanted to be friendly and get acquainted with such a man.

Mr Johnston blinked like he was coming out of his trance.

'You've done me a favour,' says he. 'You've got my thanks, son.'

'Maybe we've done each *other* a favour,' says Seth, and gave Mr Johnston a keen glance, but what Seth meant by that, I never did learn because just then the sheriff arrived. He was a brawny young man, but with white hair beginning to show in his sideburns, which had got there early on account of the worrisome nature of his job.

'I'm making no charges,' says the sheriff. 'I've heard witnesses already, and it sounds like a clear case of self-defence.'

Mr Johnston nodded. 'That's right,' says he.

'You're free to go, Mister,' says the sheriff, 'and in my judgement that's just what you should do, all three of you.'

He smiled in a mighty pleasant way. 'No offence, gentlemen but you'll have heard the saying, "Gunplay draws gunplay." In my experience that saying is a true one. Now, I aim to keep the peace round here. I don't want some young madhead trying to make his reputation on you, sir.'

'I understand,' says Mr Johnston. 'What about him?' He nodded towards the body of the little feller.

'I'll see he gets planted.'

Mr Johnston frowned at that. 'Here,' he says, taking money from his pocket. 'Would you be kind enough to give that to the undertaker?'

The sheriff looked at him, puzzled.

'See he gets a decent funeral,' says Mr Johnston, nodding towards the little feller. 'Nobody should be put under like a dog. Not even him.'

'I'll send the waggon,' says the sheriff, and tipped his hat, and went off, shaking his head.

That weren't the end of it. Mr Johnston walked over and stood by the body. He shut his eyes and I saw his lips moving. It could only be a prayer. That was when I first had Mr Johnston figured for a religious man. It struck me as a mighty civil thing to do, to offer a prayer for the repose of the soul of a feller that had been about to plug you in the back, and I said so to Mr Johnston.

'Well,' he mumbles in that strange voice of his, 'you might have to kill a man, but damnation's another kettle of fish.' He says he reckoned even the worst rat breathing was worth a prayer, just on the off-chance.

'Even a Bounty Hunter?' says Seth, looking hard at Mr Johnston.

Mr Johnston said nothing.

'Ain't that what he was?' says Seth.

'Something of the sort,' says Mr Johnston, and climbed on his horse, and soon we was riding out of Cheyenne.

'Which way are you boys heading?' asks Mr Johnston.

'We're headed north, to Montana,' says Seth. He gave Mr Johnston his nicest smile. 'You care to ride with us?'

'Why not?' says Mr Johnston. 'One place is the same as another to me these days.'

'Right then,' says Seth, looking pleased. 'That's settled.'

'Glad to have you with us,' says I.

Mr Johnston nodded and gave a shy grin but he didn't say nothing more.

That was how me and Seth first got friends with Mr Johnston and went together up the Bozeman trail to Montana. But you'll appreciate that what we'd seen that day weren't no 'slaying'; it was a fair show, which is a very different thing.

2

> . . . the two of them then fell in with the man referred to
> as Mr Johnston, to form an ominous trio. . . . Indeed, of
> the three men in question, two at least are self-confessed
> murderers.

Mr Johnson, Seth, and me

To call us an 'ominous trio' makes it sound as if we was all
cast in the same mould, which we weren't. It sounds like we
was three roughs that had teamed up just to help out with
each other's murders. In fact, we was all mighty different.
You take Mr Johnston, for instance. He was a man who
never said much. He was a brooding, melancholy sort of
feller, whereas Seth was a young rip that was always fooling
round and getting into scrapes. He was a joker, was Seth, a
joker with a pleasant smile and an easy manner, and a tongue
that could work itself round any sort of outrageous story.
Seth had plenty of gab but all the same, you never got to
know him, not deep down, whereas with Mr Johnston, it
was different. He didn't say much, but you could be sure
that what he *did* say was the truth, and gradually you could
build up a picture. As for being a self-confessed murderer,
it's true that Mr Johnston had killed men, and he was a
mighty fast hand with a gun, which I don't suppose had
come about by accident, but he was also a religious man, as
I've said, and sorely troubled in spirit about any life that he'd
been forced to take – and I believe he'd taken quite a few by

the time we teamed up. But the best way to show the sort of man Mr Johnston was would be for me to tell you his story, as I built it up from what he said.

The first thing to know about Mr Johnston is that he came from England. He spent all his young life over there, which accounted for his strange way of talking. He told me that as a young man he lived in a place called Sheffield, and that Sheffield is in Yorkshire, which is a State of England. He was working at a mill in Sheffield, and it was a monstrous hard, mean sort of existence. He says his soul got restive with it, and he was seeking round for an answer, and that's what took him along to hear the Mormon missionary that had come over to spread the Word. Mr Johnston was fairly bowled over by that missionary. He saw his life in a new light, and what rubbish it had been so far – sweating at the mill, and getting drunk, and going off with loose women. It weren't no kind of life for a man interested in salvation. The upshot was, Mr Johnston was converted, and come over to Utah. He says his heart nearly bursted with joy the first time he set eyes on the city at Salt Lake. It was such a clean place, and so pretty, with broad ways and bright streams of water, and gardens and fruit trees, and all the good land they'd brought under the ditch. Mr Johnston figured he'd struck Paradise, but it didn't turn out like that. 'Every Eden has its Serpent,' says he, and the particular Serpent in Salt Lake went by the name of Elder Price.

But before we get to Price, I figure I should say a word about the Sons of Dan, because maybe you won't have heard of them. The top Mormon at Salt Lake went by the name of Brigham Young, and he run the place with a rod of iron, and many a hundred mile of the Territory besides. Brigham Young saw that law and order was kept, and some of them laws was his own work and you couldn't find the like of them nowhere else in the entire Union. Naturally, he had to have men to enforce his laws, and these men were called the Sons of Dan, which was a fancy name taken from the Scriptures. The Mormons have a weakness for fancy names.

Mr Johnston found himself picked out to be one of the Sons of Dan, and he says they was a pretty mean bunch, in a religious way. When Brigham Young decided it was time to smite the wrongdoer and tromp the unrighteous down, it was the Sons of Dan he called on, and they rode out and did the job. Mr Johnston says he weren't entirely easy in his mind about some of the things they were ordered to do, but he buckled to it, and worked hard with his gun, till the time came when he could shade most of the others on the draw, and he saw that one of the gifts that the Lord had given him was for gunplay. 'Mormons paid their tithe in goods,' says Mr Johnston. 'All except the Son of Dan – he paid his in men!' It had to be done, he says, or the settlements would have been torn apart by all the rogues and lawbreakers that came streaming West, but it weren't work for the squeamish.

At this time, Mr Johnston had met up with a good Mormon girl by the name of Mary Oates, and the two of them was making plans to marry, but it seems Mary had been spotted by other eyes. This is where Elder Price comes into it. He was the Serpent that did the spotting, and he liked what he saw. Price made a few enquiries, and the next thing Mr Johnston knew, he'd been sent off on a job that took him away a long time and was middling dangerous. 'You remember what David ordered should be done to Uriah, that was Bathsheba's husband?' says Mr Johnston. 'The order was to put him in the forefront of the battle and get rid of him that way. I reckon that's what Elder Price had in mind for me.'

The only difference was, Mr Johnston came back alive, and when he did, Mary told him how Elder Price had approached her, and told her how it had been revealed to him from Above that he should take her for his wife. Mary was flummoxed. Naturally, she didn't want to go against the Almighty, but on the other hand she weren't very partial to Elder Price, being as he was about forty years older than her, and had a bald head, and a wart on his nose, and four wives already.

As soon as he heard this news from Mary, Mr Johnston went along to talk things out with Price. They both put their points of view, and Elder Price's point of view come out well on top. Price says Mary had been marked out for honour and exaltation in her marriage, and he backed up his words by putting armed men at her door to warn Mr Johnston off. Elder Price made a public announcement that the marriage between himself and Mary Oates would take place within the next few days, and then he sent a private message to Mr Johnston warning him not to put his shovel in no more.

Mr Johnston didn't say nothing, but on the morning of the wedding-day, he saddled up a couple of fast horses and then went along to the ceremony, wearing his guns. He broke in on the guests and held them at gunpoint. 'Go outside and mount the grey horse,' he tells Mary, and off she went. 'Anybody stir and I'll have to shoot,' he warns the guests, and they knew his reputation, and they took him seriously. Nobody moved a peg at first, but then old Elder Price got agitated. Maybe he reckoned he was under special guidance from Above again, but if so, it was bad judgement, because when he dived for a drawer and tried to get his weapon, Mr Johnston plugged him, just like he'd said he would.

Mr Johnston and Mary lit out fast, and hardly drew rein till they got to Colorado. The thing was, Mr Johnston knew that he'd be published in Utah as a renegade and a murderer, and every man's hand would be against him. That was the way it turned out: just like he'd thought, there was a price put on his head. Anyhow, he and Mary won their way clear. He says Mary was weeping one minute at being cast out by her Church and laughing the next at being with him rather than in Price's bed. After a while, she quit weeping altogether, and says she was right glad to be shot of Price, exaltation or no exaltation! Mr Johnston and Mary got married in Colorado and for a while they was happy as could be, but then she took sick of the mountain-fever, and died, and was buried outside Denver.

I guess that's when Mr Johnston got to be so melancholy. He told me he took to wondering whether Mary's death hadn't been a punishment for drilling Price. 'Mary has made her Blood Atonement,' says he, and he figured in that case he'd be next. He explained that Mormons believe there are some sins so bad they can only be washed away by the blood of the sinner, spilt upon the ground. The sinner has to die in some violent way before his sin can be forgiven. Mary had paid for her sin and Mr Johnston figured he'd be next. Not that he minded over much, he would have welcomed it, but when it came to the push, he couldn't accept it without fighting back. For instance, he'd already had a brush with the little feller that I saw him rub out in Cheyenne. The little feller was trailing Mr Johnston for the price that had been laid on his head, and as the reward was offered for him dead or alive, the little feller would have blown him through, and welcome, and Mr Johnston would have had his Blood Atonement. Well, Mr Johnston had just not been able to submit meekly and let himself be drilled or hanged. He'd got himself away, and given the little feller a bad scare into the bargain. Same thing at Cheyenne: Mr Johnston *would* fight, and if he fought, there weren't many gunhands could stand against him, so it was the little Bounty Hunter that went down, and Mr Johnston was left still waiting for his Blood Atonement to catch up with him, and sometimes, in his quieter moments, he longed for it.

I judged Mr Johnston's to be a right pitiful story, and once I'd heard it, I couldn't blame him for being somewhat on the moody side. He'd had awful bad luck and, when you thought about it, he weren't no ordinary gunslinger, but a man that came to his shooting by way of his religion. Sure, he'd killed men. He killed Price and he killed the little Bounty Hunter feller, besides what he done when he was riding with the Sons of Dan, but he weren't no murderer, and the killings lay heavy on his conscience. One thing I will say for Mr Johnston's misfortunes, they'd made him an expert with a hand-gun. Truly, he was monstrous fast.

So you see, little by little, I came to know where I was with Mr Johnston, but with Seth I never did know, not for sure. You could never pin Seth down. If he'd kept mum about himself, that would have been one thing. A man has a right to his secrets and there was fellers a-plenty out West that might never have been born in a place nor reared in a family, but just squidged up like Adam out of the prairie dust, they kept so quiet about their beginnings. Such men had their reasons, and it weren't a good idea to go prying into their secrets, not unless you had a relish for a slug of lead about your person. But that weren't the case with Seth. He'd talk, but what he said was rot. One time he'd tell you he came from Nebraska, the next from Texas. On the days when he came from Nebraska, he was an orphan child whose ma and pa had been butchered by a Sioux war-party; but when he came from Texas, his father was a rancher in a big way, running longhorns on the Panhandle. 'If that's so, why aren't you with him, then?' says I. 'Oh,' says he, 'we had a difference of opinion.' Another time, he told me he was reared in Kansas, and his pa played a big part in the troubles down there. 'Ain't you heard of Sam Walsh?' says he. 'You must have! Why, he run his own private graveyard. He was the fiercest corpse-maker in the entire Territory – and I take after him.'

'You're telling stories again, Seth,' says I.

'No,' says he. 'You got my oath on it, my Bible oath,' but he was laughing and smiling while he said it, and you knew durn well you couldn't believe a word. He'd tell you anything, would Seth, anything that tickled his fancy, and as for that Bible oath of his, it weren't worth shucks. Still, you couldn't help but like Seth, he was such fun at that time.

It was through one of Seth's jokes that we first run up against Henry Plumer – 'Handsome Henry' as they used to call him. We hadn't been settled in Montana more than a few days, and had shacked up in an old abandoned cabin near Helena, meaning to try our luck at gold-mining. We left Mr Johnston setting the cabin to rights while we rode into town for provisions, which included a visit to the saloon, if you was with Seth. That boy always had a spark in his throat! We was standing up at the bar and the talk had turned to horses when a very earnest, sincere look came over Seth's face, which should have been a warning to me.

'You ever see an Oregon Wild Horse?' says Seth. 'No, I reckon that would be outside your experience, Missouri.'

'I know all kinds of horseflesh,' says I.

'It's clear to me you don't know the Oregon. He's special. I only know about him myself because I once happened to be over that way. The Oregon's range is in the Cascade Mountains and nowhere else.'

'Oh yeah.'

'It's God's truth, Missouri. And he's the strangest crittur.'

'What's so different about him?' says I, like a fool.

'Why, even a young Oregon is higher at the shoulder than the top of a man's head. And that's a foal.'

'You're telling stories again, Seth.'

'No, I ain't. You got my oath on it, Missouri.'

'Never mind your oath.'

'I saw one only yesterday. A feller had one, not far from here.'

'Rot!' says I. 'There's no such horse.'

'Bet you twenty dollars.'

'You'll have to show me, Seth.'

'Sure!' says he, and went running out of the bar.

About twenty minutes later, I heard a rumpus in the street outside. I could hear folks laughing and hollering, and horses neighing, and over that, I could hear Seth's voice. 'Make way!' he was yelling. 'Make way for the Kansas Flyer.' It must have been one of his Kansas days.

I went out to see what he'd got, and if he weren't up on the most enormous, ugly beast I'd ever set eyes on. The crittur had a big, sneering head that it held up high in the air, it had nasty yellow teeth, and feet that it put down like plates in the dust, and two humps on its back with Seth lodged between them.

25

'There you are,' says Seth to me. 'A genuine Oregon. Pass me up my twenty bucks, Missouri.'

'I don't know what you got there,' says I, 'but it ain't no horse.'

'Sure it is. Give me my twenty.'

'It's not a horse, Seth.'

'You're just displaying your general ignorance,' says he. 'OK, I'll come down and collect my twenty.' He gave the brute a jog with his heels and it folded up like a two-foot rule, and Seth swung clear.

I stared at the thing, wallowing in the dust. 'Where the hell you come by it?' I says. 'A raree show?'

'I told you already,' says Seth. 'This horse is from Oregon.'

'Then you'd best get him back there. And fast!' says a drawling, soft-spoken voice from behind us. Both of us spun round to see who owned the voice, and we found it was Henry Plumer, sheriff of Helena. Henry was a dandy of a man, with a tail-coat and a silk vest and fine supple boots of tooled leather. He was a very quiet talker, was Henry; he had a lisp, and the funny thing was, that lisp made him sound gentle when he was fooling round, but when he was mad, it lay on his tongue like poison. Henry was a good-looking man with full red lips that he kept wetting, and bright blue eyes that bored into you. Women liked Henry Plumer a lot.

'I want that bwute out of here,' says Henry. 'They're banned. Don't you know there's a town ordinance against camels?'

'So that's a *camel*!' says I. 'Well, now, I never seen a camel before.'

'Sure it's a camel,' says Henry. 'That particular dungheap

happens to be a Bactwian camel, used for hauling fweight over the mountains. Now, young man, if your curiosity is satisfied, perhaps you could pwevail upon your fwiend to get it the hell out of here!'

'I'll take him now, sir,' says Seth. 'Right this minute.'

'Because they fwighten the horses. And when you get back, come and see me at my office,' says Henry Plumer.

I thought, by that, Seth might have got into a little trouble, but it didn't turn out that way. I don't know what story he told Henry Plumer at the office, but from that time on, the two of them became good friends, and went drinking together, and before long Henry had enrolled Seth as a Deputy.

Maybe you begin to see that Seth was a great one for jokes and stories – and he *was* a self-confessed murderer, if you went by his word, which you couldn't. One thing that made me doubt him was, he weren't all that good with a gun when I first knew him. He was a fair shooter, but not good. He could shade me at that time, but that weren't much to brag about, because I was just a farm boy that had got discontent back in Missouri and lit out for the Territories.

My story was that my pa and ma had a farm outside Belleville, and I was raised there and went to school in the village. Belleville was a mighty pretty place, as I recall, with whitewashed houses and such flowers in the gardens! Tangles of rose-vines, and honeysuckle, and morning-glories, and geranium flowers in the window-boxes, as red as blood. A pretty old place it was, lying by the bank of the river. I run around there, and was happy, and would have been there still, I reckon, except that one day when my pa was slinging sacks of meal into the waggon, he put a hand up to his chest, and groaned, and fell dead. I was there and seen it; I would have been eleven or twelve years old at the time.

Our life on the farm changed after that. We was poor, all of a sudden, and things got worse, not better. We went around looking more and more shabby until Ma solved her money problem by marrying Mr Belton, who was our neighbour on the next farm. His fences ran with ours, so it looked like a good idea all round, but Belton was a big fierce bull of a man, and my trouble was that he didn't take to me. Ma used to tell me how I must try to love Mr Belton and look on him as a father, and then the old blister would come in and whip the daylights out of me, for nothing. I took to going off, out of his way, and would stay away for days together, sleeping rough in the hay-barns or the sheds down by the tannery. Belton didn't want me around, so every time I showed up at the farm again, he'd lay into me, and Ma would sit there with her lips pressed tight together and say nothing. Belton used to say he was whipping me because I'd strayed off and lived like a beggar, and brought shame on the family. He used to say he was beating the Devil out of me, but in my opinion, he beat the Devil in.

Sometimes, in my dreams, I still see Belton, his red face looming over me, his rolled-up sleeves and hairy arms, and the stick in his hand. He starts lashing away, but in the dream, I'm heeled. Before long, I stand up and draw my weapon. . . . What actually happened was that I run away for good. To this day, I've never been back to Belleville. I lit out for the Territories, and from then on I made my own living, working at one thing or another, but I was just a farm-boy that had never even owned a gun until I met Seth.

I would have been about seventeen then, and was mule-skinning for a living. I don't know why me and Seth stuck together, but we did. I think it was that I looked up to him at that time, and Seth was never averse to being admired. I guess I was rather like a mirror to him, and he saw what a great man he was reflected in my eyes. Seth was a few years older than me, and a few years is worth a lot in terms of worship when you're seventeen. It was Seth that first called me 'Missouri' instead of my given name, which is 'Noah'. He used to call me 'The Missouri Kid' and that got shortened to 'Missouri'. It was Seth gave me the name, and it was Seth introduced me to hand-guns. We used to practise together. Seth weren't all that fast, and nor was I at that time, but we was interested in the subject.

I guess the reason why Seth was so keen to be friends with Mr Johnston was that Mr Johnston happened to be a prime hand with a gun. We asked Mr Johnston to teach us shooting, and he did. He said it was mostly practice, and never mind the fancy tricks. 'Don't bother about rolling the gun, nor fanning it, nor the Road-Agent's Switch, nor any of that flash rubbish. Keep it simple,' says he. 'That way, you'll continue breathing. And another thing,' says he. 'No man can be on the shoot and stay alive without he goes every day to the butts. You got to keep working at it, boys; you got to show ambition and persistence to be good with a gun. And remember, if you can't get the blamed gun out of the holster, you don't get the chance to fire, so practise the draw.' He said some gunhands used to grease the holster-leather and saw an inch off their gun-barrel to get a faster draw, but he didn't recommend that. He held that it was better to have the length so that you fired true, because a sawn gun was more likely to slew off target. 'Not much good being a second faster if you miss your aim,' says he. 'No, you just got to learn to get her out fast, and that takes practice. It's all in the practice, both draw and aim.'

He worked with us, and every day we put some time in, and like he said, we did get better, but we never come up to Mr Johnston, who had a fine natural talent for gunplay. One thing that happened was that I began to improve over Seth. When Mr Johnston started to teach us, Seth was maybe a fraction faster than me, but before long it was the other way round. Seth didn't like that. If I'd done some good shooting I had to pretend it was luck, for fear that Seth would take offence. He used to say things like, 'Carry on in that way, Missouri, and I'll have to call you out. One of these days, I *will* call you, and then we'll see who's the better hand with a gun.' He always said it like it was a joke, but his voice was tight underneath. Anyhow, he never did call me.

After a while, I grew more confident about my skill with guns and would sometimes go into town heeled, which was foolhardy, because if you wear guns you're announcing yourself as a man that figures he can look after himself in that respect, and sooner or later somebody's going to take you up on it, some young shooter that aims to increase his reputation by blowing you through. It was foolhardy, but I was young myself, so I done it, and sure enough, I ran into trouble. I paid a visit one night to the bar of the Eagle Hotel, which was the toniest spot in Helena by far, and I went there wearing my irons. By the end of that evening, I had killed my first man. I admit to that, but as for being a 'self-confessed murderer', I leave you to judge.

The truth was, I wanted to shine that night at the Eagle. I wanted to look my best, and maybe show a little swagger, so I donned my best shirt and polished up my boots and strapped on my gun-belt, just like any young blood might. The Eagle Hotel belonged to Mr Quarles, and it was the biggest place in town; besides the long bar, it had gaming-tables, and fiddlers on a stage at one end; it was all pretty high-class. Next to the Eagle, and joined by a connecting door, there was a cat-house, and the crib-girls from there used to get into the Eagle on the scout for custom. The girls was very discreet and so Mr Quarles used to tolerate their presence, even if he was a respectable churchgoing man. In fact, as I found out later, Quarles was the owner of the premise next door, though he didn't run the house, of course: he let the property off to others, and they ran it and paid him a stiff rent. It weren't too surprising that he should own both places because Quarles owned a heap of things round Helena – stores, saloons, and land. He had property in Bannock, too, and Virginia City, and God knows where else besides. His interests run clean through Montana, and far beyond.

Mr Quarles was what they call 'a big man', though you'd never have thought so to look at him. Although he was on the small side, he weren't no sort of build to go ranging the hills. He was fat and out of shape, and had the kind of skin you get from living mostly under oil-lamps. Mr Quarles's eyes was black as prunes, and he sported side-whiskers that joined up with his moustache. He must have been middling proud of them whiskers, because he oiled them regular with bear's grease, and was forever stroking and fingering them. He was plump as a pigeon, and wore shoes, and had the most reasonable way of talking imaginable. He always called himself a man of peace, and it was true he didn't care for fuss of any kind. He liked it best when everybody was friendly and sociable, and the cash was running into his pockets like water down a flume.

He said he aimed to keep life peaceful at the Eagle, and for a man in his position that could mean only one thing: hiring a gunhand. Not that he called the feller by that name. He says, 'I've got to have somebody to protect my interests,' but what he meant by that was a gunhand. The man that had entered his employ was a shooter by the name of Greg Carter, that had a considerable reputation round about. Greg was young, and he had one of them cat-faces, keen and staring, and his eyes was green. He sported a thin moustache that dropped below the corners of his mouth and gave him a sarcastic air, and when he walked about the Eagle, he seemed to be sneering, like he didn't think much of the customers. He thought highly of Greg Carter, though: you could see that by the black shirt with silver buttons he was wearing, and his smart grey pants that was cut tight to the leg, and his glossy boots. He thought plenty about himself, even if the rest of the world didn't come up to much. He used to stalk round the Eagle, helping himself to free liquor every now and then, and sneering at the clientele. He was always smart. His hands was soft, with pale fingers that looked like they might smell of soap; but they was lean fingers, and quick, and fit for devilries, like the rest of him. Even the way he walked and the supercilious way he smiled was like saying, 'Don't mess with me. I'm too fast.' He was a young rooster on the strut.

I'd got myself smartened up that night because of a certain young lady that I expected to see. She was an entertainer at the Eagle, and her name was Belle – I'd found that much out already. Not that I'd exchanged a word with her so far, but the last time I'd been in the Eagle, she'd come up to the bar and caught sight of me, and when I ventured a smile, she went so far as to smile back. I was young at the time, not much above eighteen, and I weren't used to fine ladies with silk dresses and shining gold hair taking an interest in me, but I liked the idea once I'd met it, and had vowed to go to the Eagle again and try to strike up an acquaintance with her.

I stood by the bar that night and watched Belle and her friend Lily do their act on stage, and in my opinion they was first-rate. They wore tall plumes in their hair and the most glittering dresses. Belle looked like a goddess, and she did the singing. Lily was a pert, black-haired little article, and she did more of the dancing. Lily pranced around and leant on her parasol, shoving out her south-end and rolling her big audacious eyes at the audience. Belle sang the accompaniment in a sweet, sad voice, sounding like an angel, even if the words was a trifle sassy. The fellers sure loved them girls, and so did Mr Quarles, because of the way they pulled in trade.

After the act, I noticed Belle come walking my way along the bar, so I plucked up my courage and I says, 'Evening, ma'am. You was really great just now,' and I tipped my hat to her.

'Thanks, mister,' she says, offhand, without looking. Then she threw a glance in my direction and saw who it was that had spoken, and she stopped and smiled at me again. I judged my luck was in at that.

'Hello,' she says. 'You again. You're getting to be a regular customer.'

'Yes, ma'am. That's my intention.'

She came and stood beside me. ' "Really great" was I?' she says, sounding as if she found my remark funny. Right from the start, Belle had this way with her, as if she was making mock of me, but only gently.

'That's right,' says I. 'Ma'am, I'd be right honoured if . . .' I dried up about there.

'Come on,' says Belle. 'Don't leave me in suspense.'

'. . . if you'd take a drink with me.'

'Sure I'll take a drink with you,' says she, 'but it'll have to be a quick one.' She gave me a big smile and leant her elbow on the bar. 'What's your name?' she asks.

'Missouri. Folks generally call me that.'

'Hi, Missouri. I'm Belle.'

'Oh, I know that already.'

'You do, eh?' We looked into each other's faces and her eyes caught mine. 'How old are you, Missouri?'

'Twenty-one,' I lied. 'Going on twenty-two.'

'A real old-timer,' she says. 'Here's mud in your eye,' and she tipped back her glass and showed her long white neck. Belle's skin was pale but it had a tender bloom to it, the kind of gleam you get on fair girls, sometimes. She was tall and stately, and her figure at that time was ample but not the least bit overblown. She was lovely, and her eyes was a clear blue. She had the kind of looks that made you think of angels. The only flaw I could find in her was her voice, which was a little hard and clipped, but then, she came from somewhere back East. Pennsylvania, I think it was. Anyhow, she asked me what I did for a living, and I told her that just at present we was trying our luck at gold-mining, and then we chatted about this and that, and I judged we was getting along fine until, on sudden, a low voice by my ear says, 'Belle, don't you know you're wanted at the office?'

Belle looked kind of flustered to be told this. 'Hello, honey,' she says. 'I was just talking to a friend.'

It was Greg, the young shooter, in his black silk shirt. 'Oh yeah?' says he, and stared hard at her, and then at me, with them cat's eyes. 'You mean this here is a *friend* of yours, Belle?' He nodded his head in my direction.

'That's right. He's called Missouri. Let me introduce you.'

'I thought he might have been bothering you,' says Greg.

'No,' says Belle. 'He hasn't. Not at all.'

'I never realized,' says Greg, slow and casual, giving us his supercilious smile, 'I never knew you was in the habit of making friends with farm-boys.'

'Excuse me, but I ain't no farm-boy,' says I, speaking out.

'I think I'll go,' says Belle. 'Goodbye, Missouri.'

'Here, wait a minute,' says I, and put my hand on her shoulder. 'I wanted to ask you . . .'

'Take your paw off her, hayseed,' says Greg.

'But I just wanted to . . .'

'Don't lean on him, Greg,' says Belle, sounding a little desperate. 'Can't you see he's harmless?'

'He shouldn't ought to come in here heeled, if he's harmless,' says Greg. 'He shouldn't go running after other folk's women, if he's harmless.'

'Now wait a minute . . .' says I.

'You talking to me, farmer boy?'

'He ain't much more than a kid,' says Belle. 'Have you been on the bottle, Greg. Is that why you're so nasty?'

'Shut your head!' says Greg. 'Or I'll shut it for you,' and he raised one of them soft lean hands like he was going to slap her down.

'Cut that out!' says I, before I knew what I was doing. My mouth had run clean out of control.

Greg turned on me, his face all smiles now that he'd got what he wanted. 'You'd better take them words back, mister,' says he. 'I should take them back right smart, if I was you.'

'You ain't me, though.'

'Don't, boys,' cries Belle. 'Please don't fight. There's no occasion for it.'

I could have told her she was only making things worse. Greg wouldn't be persuaded to back off now, not before he'd made me eat dirt. He was spoiling for trouble, and I'd had the bad luck to run up against him when I was wearing guns, and had given him an excuse by talking to Belle.

Belle called Mr Quarles over, and he came bumbling up on his patent-leather shoes, looking nervous.

'Now Greg,' says Quarles. 'I think we can settle this matter without trouble.'

He might as well have been talking to the wall. That's the problem for a man like Quarles when he hires a feller of Greg's sort: how to keep him under control. You see, a man on the shoot like Greg, he lives by his reputation, and when he gets so far into a fuss he just can't afford to crawfish out again. He might not be in a serious fight for as long as a year, but once he's started, well, he has to go on to the end, or else he won't believe in himself, in which case he wouldn't be worth hiring, not by Quarles nor nobody else.

Greg stood there, stiff-legged, glaring at me. 'All right then,' he says. 'Make your play, hayseed.'

I think he still expected me to back down. Well, I did myself, and when I realized I weren't going to back down, my heart began to thump and I was awful scared for a moment. Then, in some strange way, I came over calm. I seemed to move into a new space that was keen and watchful and still. It was the strangest feeling. I could hardly hear the racket folks made when they went scrambling out of the line of fire. The noise came to me from a considerable distance. It was like I was being pushed on by something outside myself. I was tense but cool; only my hands ached a little from knowing what was going to be expected of them.

'Make your play!' Greg says again, glaring at me, his eyes hungry.

'You make the play,' says I. 'You make the play and I'll match you.'

He sneered at that, but he didn't do nothing. We stood there and time stretched and stretched, and I knew it was bound to snap before long. Ain't it odd, I remember thinking, I don't want to kill this Greg feller, even if he has been acting poison mean; I don't want to, but it looks like I'm going to try. And suddenly, I felt mighty sharp.

He was testing my nerve with the wait but I outlasted him; it was Greg that went for his gun first. We both got off a round about the same time. His creased my neck, but I felt nothing at the time, save a touch like a feather. Then I saw him stagger and go down. He fell like he'd been poleaxed, and his guns went clattering away. It was amazing to me that I could have been responsible for such a change in him. I saw I hadn't hit where I aimed. Somehow I had dragged my shot down and the slug had struck him in the crook of the thigh. A red soak showed on his smart grey pants. I stood there with my guns still levelled on him, feeling sleepy and let down all of a sudden. I could hardly remember how sharp I'd felt a moment before.

There was a buzz from the crowd. A voice said, 'That young stranger, he got Greg.'

'Hellfire, he took him fair and square!' says another.

Belle went and stooped over Greg. Then she turned sorrowful blue eyes on me and says, 'You think he's going to be all right?'

'He'll live,' says I. 'Bind up his wound till the surgeon gets to him and he'll probably be OK.'

I watched Belle take the silk wrap off her shoulders and tie it round the top of his thigh.

Greg peered up at me with them cat's eyes, but their light had faded some. 'Who *are* you?' he says. 'Because, man, you're fast!'

'I ain't nobody,' says I. 'Nor are you, Carter.'

He hung his head on hearing that.

'I want to apologize,' says Mr Quarles, coming buzzing up like a bee. 'I want to tender you my apologies for this unfortunate incident . . .'

He went on in that vein but I weren't really listening. I was feeling sorry for Greg Carter, of all things. I was feeling sad to see him lying there, with his blood oozing through the silk wrap, and his reputation gone. He was finished as a gunfighter in Helena, and he weren't even dead. It was strange but I felt a sight nearer to Greg than I did to Quarles, and yet he'd just tried to kill me. 'Listen,' says I to Greg, 'You shaded me on the draw, but your shot run off.' I put up a hand and touched my neck and it come away wet.

Quarles was still blatting away in my ear: 'I can't think what come over Mr Carter to do that,' he says. 'I can't understand it at all. . . .'

'You got the barrel sawn?'

'A little,' says Greg.

'Well,' I says, 'it don't always pay.'

'I *knew* you was somebody,' says Greg, and sighed, and closed his eyes.

'My profound apologies . . .' says Quarles. 'I want to ask you to step up and have a drink on the house.'

'Thanks, Mr Quarles. I will.' I certainly needed a drink by that time.

A couple of bartenders carried Greg away, then one of

them came back with a bucket and spread sawdust over the patch of blood on the floor. It was only a little patch, for what had happened. I stood at the bar, gathering myself and staring at the full glass of whisky in front of me. It looked right inviting but I was a while before I ventured to pick it up. I had a feeling my hand might shake and spill the liquor over the counter for the barman to have to swab up, and shame me in that way. But when I did take hold of the glass, I found my grip was tolerable steady.

I think it was the same night that Mr Quarles came up with his proposition. He says Greg Carter would be on his back a long while, and anyhow he was no good for the job any more, having been beat. To tell the truth, says Quarles, it had come as a blessed relief, all things considered, that he had gone down to my gun. He had become uppity and overbearing lately till there weren't no dealing with him. Mr Quarles says he hadn't no time for a man that couldn't keep to his instructions, then he asked me if I would like Greg Carter's position. At first, I laughed out loud at the idea of me as a gunhand, but Quarles offered me good pay and pressed me hard, and in the end I took on – though as you may be able to guess, it weren't for Quarles and his money. It was so I had a reason to be near Belle every night: I had fallen hard for that young woman.

About a week later it must have been, I was in the Eagle filling my new position and I was joshing with Belle, and I said something about Greg Carter to the effect that at least I'd saved her from getting her face slapped.

'Don't joke on that subject,' says she.

'Why not, Belle?' says I, still joking. 'Don't you like to feel beholden?'

'Greg's dead,' she says. 'That's why!'

'Dead? What do you mean, dead?' I stuttered. 'He can't be.'

'The gangrene got into his wound and he's dead. They're burying him tomorrow.'

Nobody could have been more astounded than me. But I ask you, did the fact that Greg died make me a murderer? Nobody thought so at the time – in fact, I attended the funeral.

3

... giving him employment and encouraging him to
lead a decent and regular life.

Working at the Eagle

That's how I was given employment: Quarles hired my gun
to keep the peace in the Eagle, and being as I'd established
my reputation by rubbing out the previous holder of the
position, poor feller, I didn't have too much trouble. If the
boys got too uproarious, it was my job to persuade them
that it would be a lot more fun to shoot out the lights at the
next place down the street, and mostly they responded to a
word of advice. As I got to know the customers, so the job
got easier, and soon I was acquainted with a lot of the fellers
that came into the Eagle, and had their respect.

It was a new experience for me at eighteen to have
anybody's respect, and it learnt me some about the ways by
which a man can make his voice heard in this world. It
struck me you could gain attention in different ways. For
instance, there was the brand of attention men gave to
preachers, so that the words of a green young preacher might
be listened to with respect by an old man because that
preacher was judged to have the power of the Lord behind
him. Then there was the attention men gave to a young
shooter like me; men didn't argue with me because of the
power of my reputation for gunplay. Strongest of all was
the attention men paid to Mr Quarles, because of the power

of his money. Maybe Quarles was a little fat man, but he was the strongest. For instance, he could hire me, but I couldn't hire him. In every case, it struck me, the trick was made to work by means of a man's reputation. Folks didn't tangle with a preacher because he had the reputation of being the mouthpiece of the Lord; they didn't cross me because of my reputation with a gun; and they did what Quarles said because he had a reputation as a rich man that owned a deal of property. But in every case, it would only work so long as folks believed in the reputation. If they'd have challenged us, we'd have gone down, all three; even Quarles would have gone down, because folks had got to *let* him own all that money and property he was stuffed with, if you see what I mean. The truth is, folks don't realize; they can't get together on a thing, and they give too much credit to the claims of men of reputation. Just as well they do, or I shouldn't have held down my job long at the Eagle. I should have resigned, or gone out feet first, I reckon.

I got to know Belle, like I'd hoped, and I became acquainted with her friend, Lily, too. They was a right lively pair of girls. Lily was the more reckless of the two; she'd throw remarks out right and left, and toss her black ringlets, and joke with the customers in the sassiest way, and they loved it, and slapped their thighs, and declared what a young heller she was. Belle's nature was more quiet, but she could put on a flirty manner when she wanted, and a sharp tongue and a mocking laugh, as well. But there was more pride in Belle's nature; you could see it in the way she carried herself. Lily was a pert young thing, and wilful as an unbroken filly, but Belle was more queenly, or that's how it seemed to me at the time, though I weren't entirely impartial.

There was something strange in the way Belle acted

towards me. She seemed to like me, right off, and would pet me and make a fuss over me, if I allowed it, which I couldn't very well do in the bar, on account of my reputation. She'd stroke my hair, too, and that was absolutely all right with me, provided it weren't too public. Lily used to laugh when she saw us together, and ask Belle if she was sickening for something, but Belle never took no notice. 'You're the best of them,' Belle would say in her softest voice. 'You're the nicest guy around. Missouri, you're my real *beau*.' Naturally, I liked to hear such words, coming from the young woman I was stuck on, but the way she said it, somehow it was like she was talking to a kid. Maybe I was smitten but I weren't blind to that.

Seth and Henry Plumer used to come into the Eagle, regular. They said it was to see that the peace was being kept, but I judged it was more to see Belle and Lily. They hung around there pretty much and was often chatting with the two girls, and it struck me how different Belle was in their company. When they was there, Belle would joke in a hard voice, and make cutting remarks, and put on a brassy laugh. 'My God,' she says to me, once they'd gone, 'if them two aren't a couple of outrageous swaggerers!' but I saw that she and Lily always made them welcome. Belle said they had to, by the nature of their job: they was under orders from Quarles to be nice to the sheriff. I wanted to believe what she said, and so I did believe it. At eighteen, you can believe plenty.

Somebody else that I got to know by working at the Eagle was Arthur. He was a young half-breed who used to hang round the kitchens. I saw the boy there in his rags and it set me thinking. They told me he used to sleep nights in an empty bacon crate, and I was reminded of how things had stood with me a few years back, when Belton used to lay into me every time he felt the lack of entertainment, and I'd run away and lived rough. I was curious about Arthur and I asked Mr Quarles about him.

'Oh,' says Quarles, 'well, the arrangement is that I let him pick through the left-overs. You know what he was doing when I first found him? He was rummaging through the trash-cans like a famished bear. "Hey," says I. "You take my grub, boy, you'd better work for it." '

'Grub?' says I. 'As a rule, trash-cans don't hold much in the way of grub, Mr Quarles.'

'Maybe not for you nor me,' he says, 'but they do for him!'

That's the thing about fellers like Quarles: they keep all such differences in mind.

'Anyhow,' says Quarles, 'I set him to washing dishes. That's what he does, and I give him scraps and let him sleep in the shed.'

'Nice of you to trouble yourself about the boy's welfare,' says I, keeping my voice flat.

'I like to think I'm not uncharitable,' says Quarles, and – you have to believe me! – the old blister meant it. It was the same as when he talked to me once about why he'd called his place the Eagle Hotel. 'I've done it,' says he, 'because the Eagle is a symbol of our glorious United States of America. I called it by that name to show the love I bear my country,' and looked at me, all solemn, and nodded his head. I don't know about Quarles loving America, though he said it most sincere, what I do know is that he sure wanted his hands on a piece of it, and the bigger the better. He even talked in the same style about Lily and Belle. 'I hold myself responsible for them,' he used to say. 'They aren't bar-girls nor any kind of loose female, but *bona fide* entertainers, and respectable young ladies. I consider it my moral duty to look after them.' He told me how he always kept a fatherly eye on them – but I judged it was more like the kind of eye a man keeps on his banker – them two girls was a big success with the customers, and he knew it. But that was the way Mr Quarles talked: he was a master of high-flown rot.

Arthur sure was raggedy, and his face was yellow, and he smelt a little high in hot weather, but I liked him. I had a soft spot for that boy. Folks said he was gone in the head and sometimes they would take advantage of his simple nature. Their idea of providing themselves with a little fun was to tell Arthur that there was a ghost after him, which was sure to scare him into fits. He'd hide himself away then, and you'd have hell's own job to get him to come out. I tried to explain to Arthur that they was only fooling him, but he never learnt. He was just plumb terrified of ghosts and spirits. I guess it was his Injun blood coming out in him.

I took Arthur with me for a treat one day when I was going to see Mr Johnston. I went to the cabin most afternoons and put in a little time on our claim, because I was still a partner with Seth and Mr Johnston, even if I didn't work the claim so much now. I always looked on my position at the Eagle as temporary, and wouldn't have taken on such a job, but for the one reason that I mentioned.

Seth was still living at the claim but he weren't there when we arrived. Mr Johnston told me that Seth kept going off more and more frequent, and always with the excuse that he had private business to attend to. The truth was, Seth didn't care for steady work any more than I did myself; what he craved for was excitement. Anyhow, I introduced Arthur to Mr Johnston and them two got along fine, right from the word 'go'. It wasn't long before Arthur was helping Mr Johnston with his work, and I must say it was funny to see them together. They didn't hardly exchange a word – neither of them was what you'd call a big talker – but they did seem to have some sort of understanding going for them.

A little later, Seth rode into camp. He looked around, lifted his eyebrows, gave a smile, and says, 'What's that?' pointing to Arthur. 'Hellfire! He's got a face like a yellow-jacket!'

'That's Arthur,' says I. 'He's all right. You be nice to him!' And I told Seth how the boy lived and all.

'Is that so?' says Seth. 'A breed, ain't he?'

'He's all right.'

'The Injun come out strong in him.' Seth stared at Arthur and then at me with them soft brown eyes of his, and then he says, right gentle, 'What you want to go bringing rubbish like that into camp for?'

'You be nice to him. You hear?'

'Sure, Missouri,' says Seth, and dismounted and strolled over to the boy. When he got up to him, he says in a loud voice, 'Howdy, Yellow-Jacket.'

'Huh?' says Arthur, his eyes bugging out in surprise.

'What's your name, boy?'

'His name's Arthur,' says Mr Johnston, and gave a thoughtful spit.

'Halfer? OK, Halfer. Glad to know you,' says Seth, and after that he was all right with the boy, but he just had to have a little fun with him first.

On our way home that evening, Arthur says to me, 'Why does Seth call me "yellow-jacket" when I ain't got no yellow jacket?'

'Don't trouble your head about that,' says I. 'That's only Seth's way.'

Seth stayed on friendly terms with Arthur, but I couldn't altogether trust him not to have a little fun at the boy's expense, if I happened to be out of the way. For instance, the one time Arthur wandered into camp when I weren't there, he ended up drunk. By the time I arrived, the boy, was tighter than a tick. I had my suspicions that Seth might have given him the bottle just to get a few laughs, but when I tackled Seth about it, he swore the boy had sniffed out the bottle for himself and gone for it in true Injun style. Every bad thing about that boy his Injun blood got blamed for.

'Anyhow,' says Seth, 'as to him being drunk, what the hell's it matter? He's had a good time and now he'll sleep it off. Let him have his good times. Why not? Arthur ain't got so many good times coming that he can afford to pass any up.'

I didn't say no more. I knew what Seth meant.

You won't believe this, but Seth used to act sore about me getting the job at the Eagle. He told me how he figured he should have had it, being as he could beat me on the draw, (or so he said). 'I'm going to come into the Eagle one night and call your bluff, Missouri,' says he, smiling. 'I'll come and kick up a commotion that you can't ignore.'

'Hell,' says I. 'You wouldn't do that to an old friend.'

'It'd serve you right for working under false pretences,' says he. 'When you *know* I'm the better man.'

'According to that, Mr Johnston ought to have the job,' says I. 'Being as he can beat either of us.'

'That old freak,' says Seth. 'He'd scare the customers away. My God, ain't he getting peculiar these days. He never hardly speaks. Goes round looking blue and miserable.'

I'd noticed it myself. Poor old Mr Johnston, he was brooding on the past, and his conscience was grinding at him. He'd been talking to me about the Blood Atonement again, and he gave me such a strange look, I thought at the time he was going to ask me to spill his blood and get it over, being as we was such good friends.

'Anyhow,' says I to Seth, 'I should have thought you'd enough on as a Deputy. There looks to be work a-plenty with the road-men.'

That was a sore point in Helena at the time. There was a gang of road-men that was holding up the stages out of town and generally terrorizing the district, and it didn't seem like Henry Plumer and his Deputies could get on terms with them. Henry and his men rode out often enough, but the robbers always got away. Henry was smart enough in other directions, and kept the peace in town so that there was no complaints on that score, and hanged a man every now and then for stealing horses, but he just couldn't seem to come near that road-gang. They appeared to have mighty good information and only hit those stages that was carrying shipments of gold. Folks agreed it was downright uncanny, and top citizens like Mr Quarles that were suffering 'grievous losses', as they called it, they started to get restless. Some folks said that Henry Plumer spent too much time enjoying himself at such places as the Eagle, but none of them said it to his face, which was good judgement.

It's true that he and Seth was often in the Eagle, and it was becoming more and more easy to see why. Like I've already said, Henry was a favourite with the ladies, and it looked like Lily was no exception to the rule. Her face would light up whenever Henry walked into the room, and Belle spent middling time with Seth and Henry, too.

One day Belle told me that she and Lily was going to a private dinner-party with Seth and Henry Plumer, that was to be held in one of the upper rooms at the Eagle.

'I thought Mr Quarles had made a rule against you girls doing that?' says I.

'So he has,' says she, 'generally speaking, but he's allowing it tonight as a special favour to the sheriff.'

'Favour? What for?'

'Some kind of celebration,' says Belle, staring into my face. 'You aren't mad at me, are you, Missouri?'

'No.'

'Mr Quarles insisted. He says it's only good sense to accommodate the sheriff.'

' "Accommodate?" ' says I. 'What the hell is that supposed to mean?'

'Nothing much,' says she. 'Just provide a little feminine company. You're sure you ain't mad at me, Missouri?'

'No.'

'I tell you, it don't mean shucks, honey. You can come along if you like. How about that? Will you come if I take you?'

'I should look a rare sap – number five at a foursome!'

'Don't be sore at Belle,' says she. 'Belle ain't particular about going, either. Why *don't* you come along?'

'I ain't going,' says I, 'and that's final.' I mean, how could I have barged in there? But as things turned out, I did get into the upper room at the Eagle that night, and this is how.

I was at my station, keeping an eye on the bar and the tables, when in busts a feller, all caked with dust and breathing heavy. 'Sheriff!' he yells. 'Is Sheriff Plumer around? It's urgent.'

'Here,' says I, 'Come with me, brother. I'll take you straight to the sheriff.' And I led him up the stairs and along the corridor to where I knew the supper-party was taking place. We could hear them from some way off, there was such a deal of laughing and merry-making, and bottles clinking. I knocked on the door and walked straight in, being as it was urgent, and there they were, all sitting around, their faces flushed with liquor. Henry Plumer was there in his vest, with his coat slung over the back of his chair. He was grinning and puffing on a cigar, and young Lily was sprawled across his knee. Her cheeks looked hectic, as bright as if they'd been painted, and she was giggling and crying out, 'Tell me, Henry. What come next? Oh, I'll die laughing! Tell us what come next, you monster!'

Belle was sitting there with a strange little smile on her face. Next to her was Seth, and he was smiling, too, but they weren't touching at all, just sitting and watching the performance between Lily and Plumer.

'What's the idea, kid?' growls Henry as I walked in. He looked as savage as a meat-axe, and bit hard on his cigar. 'You know better than to bust in on folks, don't you?'

I waved the other feller forward and he told how there'd been another stage hold-up at Three Pine Creek, and the guard shot, and a gold shipment made away with. It was a pretty disastrous story.

Plumer cussed and drove Lily off his knee, though she clung to him. Surely he weren't going now? she says. Surely he would send along a Deputy instead? 'Don't be a fool,' says Plumer and got up anyhow. He just dumped Lily down in the chair and she sprawled out across the arm of it.

'A great pity, ladies,' says Henry, slinging on his coat, 'but we can't stay. Duty calls.'

Belle leant across. 'Miss Lily,' she says. 'I've got a fine view of your garter.'

'If that's all you've got a view of,' says Lily, bridling.

'Duty calls,' says Plumer again. He gave Seth a keen glance. 'It's calling you too, Deputy Walsh. On your feet, boy.'

Seth sighed, but he did as he was told, and followed Henry Plumer out of the room. 'Wait a minute,' yells Lily, and she runs after them.

Belle sat on. 'Well,' she says. 'Have a drink, Missouri. No sense in letting it go to waste.' I saw her eyes looked uncommon bright.

'To tell the truth, I ain't sure I want a drink. Not from this table.'

'Oh dear,' says Belle. 'Missouri's on his high horse. Don't sulk – it spoils your looks, honey. Come and sit by me. Come on!'

Well, I went, and she commenced to run her fingers through my hair. Then she says in a dreamy voice. 'Maybe that Plumer's a big man, but there are times when he sure can act tolerable cheap.' She gave a little sigh. 'You know what I like best, Missouri? I like best to have you beside me. Do you like that?'

By this time I was won over. 'Belle,' says I, 'this is perfect. I wouldn't want to be nowhere else but here.'

'You're such a sweet boy,' she says. 'I wish . . .'

'What do you wish, Belle?'

She began to laugh again. 'My salvation!' says she. 'If Henry Plumer ain't the most unlikely sheriff I ever heard of.'

'What do you think of Seth?'

'Seth? He can drink his share of whisky. I know that.'

'Yep,' says I. 'He's death to a bar, is Seth.'

'Good-looking feller.'

'I guess so.'

'But you're better, Missouri. Oh, I just love to see you with that long hair a-swishing round your collar. You got lovely hair.'

'So have you, Belle. I was thinking – about Lily.'

'What about Lily?'

'She seemed so . . . wild tonight.'

'Nothing wrong with Lily but for one thing,' says Belle, leaning close to me so I could feel her warm breath on my cheek. 'Our little Lily is tight. She's drunk. But no need to worry. She can put herself to bed.' Having said that, Belle planted a kiss on my mouth, and we went on from there. Later, she took me along to her room – and that was the first time Belle and me come together. To tell the truth, it was the first time I'd done it at all. I'd got to eighteen, but I was shy with women. It's strange when you think back; I'd killed a man but I'd never gone with a lady. I was a green hand at the loving business, but as it turned out, Belle and me got along fine, and afterwards I lay in Belle's arms and told her that I loved her, and she run her fingers in my hair and says, 'You're my *real* sweetheart, Missouri.'

I lay there, and I thought what a huge stroke of luck it had been that Seth and Handsome Henry should have been called away that evening. I felt so lucky when I thought of it, I laughed outright.

After that, I used to visit Belle in her room sometimes, but we always had to be careful. She explained to me that Quarles would be furious if he found out. He had a strict rule against the girls entertaining in their rooms, and if he got to hear of it he might even turn her out of the job, so we daren't go there too often. I used to get riled sometimes when

Belle wouldn't let me come up, and I'd cuss Quarles for a sanctimonious old sharp, spoiling things with his religious notions, but I soon found out Quarles was different from that.

I couldn't figure it then, and I'm not sure I can figure it now, but I'll tell you what I found. I should mention that Quarles had a room right next to Belle's, which added a little spice of adventure to my visits. Well, one night when I was paying a late call and groping my way along the corridor in the dark, I must have took the wrong door by mistake. Anyhow, I found myself in a strange parlour. There was nobody there, but the lamp was burning. I was just going to back out again when I saw some things laid out on the table, and they was so strange that I couldn't help but pause and give them a closer look. You might not believe this, but there was a shirt with a hole drilled in it, and all the material round stained with old blood. There was a silk blouse, ripped by a knife, and the silk was bloody, too. There was a length of tarred hempen rope, with a nasty-looking noose at the end of it, and there was a pair of grey pants with a dark stain on the left thigh that I was sure I'd seen before. I cast round in my mind, and then it came back to me. What in the nation was Mr Quarles doing with an article like Greg's pants? They were the same ones he was wearing when I plugged him, and Mr Quarles hadn't even bothered to get them washed. There was the hole where the bullet went in and the gangrene followed. I could see more stuff hanging on the walls, such as hats and spurs, and some pictures, too, and such things as reward posters with drawings of mighty rough-looking customers that was wanted for robbery and murder.

I couldn't figure it, but the feel of the place made me

jumpy and I didn't hang around for long. I didn't say nothing to a soul about what I'd found, but I used to ask myself what Mr Quarles wanted with such stuff, and I couldn't come up with an answer. Not until one day I walked into Quarles's office – not the private parlour – at two o'clock in the afternoon, of all blessed times, and there he was, wearing the bloody shirt, which was a sight too large for him, and with the noose round his neck. He was being dragged back and forth, up and down the room on the end of the rope by a strapping young crib-girl called Marlene, who was in her drawers and not much else. She had the rope in her hands and she was tugging him along like he was a stubborn mule, and he was groaning and squeaking and generally carrying on.

I was rooted to the spot.

'Damn,' says Quarles. 'I was under the impression I'd locked that door.' He sure looked ridiculous with the shirt flapping round his bare legs. He took off the noose, and give me a shifty glance.

'You all right, Mr Quarles?' I asks.

'Don't worry, Missouri,' says he. 'It's nothing.' His face was shiny with sweat. 'Cut along, now, dear,' he says to Marlene. 'And thank you for your help.'

The girl slung on her dress and left in a hurry.

'Well,' says Quarles, when she was out of the room, 'I guess this must look a little peculiar . . .'

'It does, Mr Quarles.'

He nodded and stroked his side-whiskers. 'Yes, it must seem that way to you, Missouri – and yet there's a perfectly natural explanation. I only put up with this type of treatment on the prescription of my doctor, I can assure you of that.'

'You don't say! What's the trouble, Mr Quarles?'

'It's – arthritis,' says he. 'Arthritis of the neck-bone. I'm a martyr to it, Missouri. The treatment is intended to, ah, loosen up the various joints.'

He gave me this line of blatt with a straight face, and I acted just as serious back to him: 'Yes, Mr Quarles,' I says, 'and I reckon it works, too. But I'm sorry to hear of your ailment.'

He nodded, kind of approving at my words, as if I'd shown good judgement. 'One thing, Missouri,' says he, in his friendliest voice. 'I shouldn't like it to be generally known that I'm afflicted with the arthritis. It's so ageing. You get me?'

'Sure. I get you.'

'Good boy! So I'd take it as a big favour if you kept this to yourself.'

'I will, Mr Quarles,' says I, and I did, except that I mentioned it to Belle, because I just *had* to talk about it to somebody.

'What do you think he's fooling round at?' says I to her, when I'd given her the story.

She shrugged. 'Maybe he *has* got the arthritis,' she says.

'No, that's not it. If it was the arthritis, why should he be wearing a dead man's shirt?'

'Search me!' says Belle, a little snappish all of a sudden.

'Ain't it a facer?'

'Hmph!' says Belle. 'I don't want to talk about such things. What girl was it, did you say?'

'Marlene.'

'That one! Why, she's as common as a barber's chair!'

'Where the hell do you think he gets hold of such things, anyway?' says I.

She tossed her head. 'Maybe the sheriff passes them over to him.'

'You mean Plumer?' I was stumped. 'Why should Sheriff Plumer want to do that?'

'Who knows?' says Belle. 'Maybe he wants to accommodate Quarles a little.'

'You mean that? I can hardly believe it.'

'I'm not sure,' says Belle quickly. 'I'm only guessing, and I expect I'm wrong.'

'I should think you are.'

'Anyhow,' says she, very hoity-toity, 'I don't want to discuss such subjects any longer, *if* you don't mind.'

'OK,' says I, and let the matter drop, and things carried on at the Eagle just the same as ever.

That's how it was when Mr Quarles first 'gave me employment and encouraged me to lead a decent and regular life'.

4

... the summary justice that was, at length, handed out to the notorious Sheriff Plumer by an infuriated populace.

A Monstrous Shock and a Close Call

Things jogged along in Helena for a fair while without much change, and then one day Handsome Henry Plumer that had seemed so confident and so much in charge, he took a fall; a bad one; the worst kind. I had no inkling of what was coming, it just burst over me like a summer storm, and it must have taken Seth the same way. This is how it happened:

Me and Seth was riding into town one day, and I had young Arthur up with me on the saddle, taking him back from one of his visits to the claim. We started up the main street of Helena, and as soon as we hit that street, it was clear that something was very wrong. The whole place was deserted. Ed Wallace, the blacksmith, had gone from his forge, the stores was standing empty and the saloons was silent as graveyards. We rode on a little way and all we saw was one feller in the distance, running like mad, with what appeared to be a rifle in his hand. Then, as we swung round the bend in the road, we could see a big crowd up ahead.

'What in the nation's going on?' says I.

'So long, Missouri,' says Seth. 'I'm branching off here.'

'Ain't you going to see what the fuss is all about?'

'Maybe I will later,' says he. 'I got a little private business to attend to first.'

'OK. See you,' says I.

Seth gave me a nod and a smile, then turned his horse's head and went trotting away down a side-alley.

Me and Arthur pushed on to see what was afoot. The crowd was a real big one and as we got nearer we could see it was gathered round a waggon. There was two men sitting up on the waggon. To the left of the waggon there was a cart, and standing on the boards of that cart was three fellers that looked to have their hands tied behind them, and all round the cart was a ring of armed men, like nobody was taking any chances.

When I got a little closer, I had a monstrous shock. The middle one of them three prisoners on the cart was Handsome Henry Plumer – though he didn't look any too handsome at that minute. Henry was gritting his teeth in fury, the blood had left his face, and even his lips that were normally so full and red had gone ashen pale. I knew the men on either side of him to be a couple of his Deputies, and they made a sorry sight. The face of one of them was all yellow and ghastly, and as for the other, his skin had come out in blotches and his mouth was hanging loose, save that now and then he twisted it into a cringing smile. There they was, the three of them, surrounded by the infuriated populace, and I guess they knew what was coming to them.

I had another big shock when I turned my eyes from the cart to the waggon: one of the two men sitting up there in judgement was Mr Quarles! I could see it was him, but at first I couldn't believe it. He looked different from his usual self. For one thing, he looked bigger: I guess he was all swole up with passion like a frog. He was sweating and mopping his brow and glaring across at Plumer, as if to say, 'No man makes a fool of me for ever!' The other judge beside him was Dr Mace, that had set up practice in the town not long before; Dr Mace was a big, stony-faced man with a frown like a thunderhead. He always wore a tall hat, and he was wearing it now.

Mace stood up and began to spout, once he'd got the crowd quiet: 'This that we've convened here is a People's Court.'

'This here is a farce!' snarls Henry Plumer.

Mace took no notice of the interruption. He just went straight on: 'Is it the People's will that we try the prisoners before us?'

'Aye!' roars the crowd. They was infuriated, all right, and it looked like Henry and his men wouldn't stand a chance.

'How the hell can you twy the shewiff?' yells Plumer, sounding desperate. 'I'm the only sort of law there *is* in Helena.'

'We can, and we will,' says Mace. 'You banked on that, Mister Plumer!'

'Listen,' says Henry. 'I'm up for considewation right now as United States Marshal to police this entire stwetch of Territory...'

'Then we'd best stop you now, before you hatch out proper,' says Mace.

'But don't that speak for my chawacter?' yells Henry, and would have gone on and said more, but one of the guards shoved his gun into Henry's face and snarls, 'Shut your head!' and Henry looked into the muzzle of that gun and he corked up, despite himself. Some of the crowd laughed to see it, but not me.

'Come on, Arthur,' says I. 'This ain't no place for a boy. I'll take you back to the Eagle.'

We was just leaving, when two riders come cantering up, running a man between them. The poor feller was scrambling along in a cloud of dust.

'Hey,' yells one of the riders. 'Here's another good friend of Plumer's we got on this rope. Ten to one he was in on it!'

'Set him aside,' says Mace. 'We'll consider his case, after.'

They dragged their captive up to the waggon, and tied him to the waggon wheel, and made all secure. The captive raised his head and spat, and I looked at that face, streaked with dirt and sweat, and my heart began to beat like a drum. It was Seth they'd got!

'Listen,' say I to Arthur. 'Take my horse. Ride to the claim. Ask Mr Johnston to come here. You got that? Ask him to come here quick. Plenty quick!'

Arthur climbed on my horse and away he went.

I could see Seth peering round among the faces of the crowd. I caught his eye and slipped him a little signal by tipping my hat back, and if you can believe it, he gave me a smile. Yes, he managed a smile, which showed considerable sand on his part, with the infuriated populace howling round him like wolves.

'All right,' yells Mace. 'Let's have order!'

The crowd fell quiet.

'These men before you,' Mace goes on, 'these men were taken red-handed in the act of holding up a stage-coach. Word was passed beforehand to the officers of the Vigilance Committee, and we layed for these men, and we took them. Unfortunately, before we could intervene, they had loosed off their guns at the driver of the coach, Jed Murphy, and he lay butchered in the dirt. Mr Murphy's body is now reposing at Pike's, the undertakers, and if any of you gentlemen care to go along and examine the deceased, you'll find proof positive of my words. The deceased is riddled with holes, having received a veritable fusillade of lead to face and body. We were, unhappily, witnesses of this slaying, and immediately after it was perpetrated, we arrested the scoundrels responsible, so there can't be a shadow of doubt but what they did it. There stand the men – on that cart!' Mace pointed an accusing finger at Henry and his Deputies. 'What's more,' he goes on, sounding unstoppable, 'we have reason to believe that most, if not all, of the highway robberies that have plagued us this past eighteen months can be laid at their door, or at the door of their associates. Plumer ran them, and what's more, he did it under cover of enforcing the law – which is about as lowdown as a man can get!'

'Who was it sold us?' calls Henry Plumer in that soft voice of his. 'Show us your man, if he ain't scared.'

'Certainly. Step forward, Mr Jacklin.' It was Quarles that did the talking this time, his voice sounding high and sharp.

'Jacklin!' says Henry. 'So you was the Judas!'

'Yeah, I done it,' says Jacklin, who was a thin, dried-out sort of man with greying hair and a scraggly neck; and you could hear in Jacklin's tone of voice that an old score was being paid off.

'Put your evidence to the People,' says Quarles, and Jacklin told the crowd how he worked Rattlesnake Farm up in the hills, and how he had been forced to let Plumer's gang use it as a hide-out.

'That's a lie,' says Henry Plumer. 'You was never forced.'

Jacklin looked middling flustered at that, and swore that he'd *had* to do it.

'You're a lying dog,' says Henry Plumer. 'You was in on the whole dodge.'

Jacklin began to sweat profuse. He swore again that he'd been forced to harbour them, and that when they came to him, he'd been too scared to say 'No'.

'Why was that?' asks Quarles.

'Because if I'd refused,' says Jacklin, 'they'd have gunned me down, like they've done plenty more.'

Henry tried to break in again, but the crowd wouldn't let him speak. They jeered him down, and the guard shoved the muzzle of his gun practically into Henry's ear, so Henry gave it up as a bad job.

Jacklin went on to put the finger on three more members of the Plumer gang, but Seth's name weren't among them, which was a considerable relief.

'We've sent out parties to arrest all three,' says Quarles in his high, excited voice. 'The Vigilance Committee is going to ensure that you good people don't have to stand any more grievous losses at their hands.'

The crowd gave a roar at that, and the loafers and free-loaders roared loudest of all.

'Now,' says Mace, taking over again, 'as your representatives and the Assessors of this People's Court, we've conferred together already, and arrived at our verdict. We find these men guilty of murder and highway robbery. Right, Mr Quarles?'

'Yes,' says Quarles, running his tongue over his lips. 'That's correct.'

'Do the sovereign People support our verdict? All in favour say "Aye".'

'Aye!' The sovereign People weren't in no doubt. Their blood was up.

'Anybody to the contrary?' says Mace, offhand, like the question was barely worth asking.

Nobody opened their mouth. You could have heard a pin fall.

The Deputy with the blotchy face gave a sob at that, and tears crept down his grey and purply cheeks.

'You, the People,' says Mace, 'have got the last word about the punishment fitting for these scoundrels. All that are in favour of hanging, raise the shout of "Aye".'

'Aye!' from hundreds of throats.

'Anybody against?'

Dead silence.

'You, the condemned,' says Mace, 'are sentenced to be hanged forthwith. If you've got anything to say, now's your chance to say it.'

'This ain't the law,' says Henry Plumer. 'As your legal shewiff . . .'

He got no further. They jeered him down.

'We've not come here to argue the law with killers, and men that betray their trust,' says Quarles. 'I vote we get on with it.'

He got a cheer for that.

'Just a minute,' says Mace. 'Is there any of the condemned willing to testify about that man?' – he pointed to Seth – 'Anybody that can say whether or not he was a party to their crimes?'

Henry Plumer curled his lip and gave Mace a ghastly sneer by way of a reply. The yellowy Deputy was in a daze and just went on looking at his boots, but the blotchy-faced one made a strangled noise.

'Yes?' says Mace. 'Speak out, man!'

'Would you ... will you ...' stammers the blotchy Deputy, '. . . can you offer me my life . . . if I speak?'

'We can't *promise* nothing,' says Mr Quarles, very severe.

The blotchy Deputy seemed bewildered by that, and stood there hesitating, with his mouth hanging open. Just then, Henry Plumer turned his head and spat full in the blotchy Deputy's face. It took a good man to be able to spit at all just then – I know my mouth was dry as hay – but Henry Plumer done it. That finished the blotchy feller. He hung his head and groaned, and when they asked him again if he'd anything to say, he wouldn't answer.

This performance of his disgusted the crowd. 'Get them to the tree!' they started yelling. 'No more talk. Let's have some action!'

'What about him, then?' shouts a big, bearded miner, pointing at Seth. 'Why don't we string him up along with them? It'll save time.'

'No!' yells Mace. 'This man's not been tried yet, and besides, there ain't room on the cart. His case comes on next.'

The shout rose then: 'Every man to the tree! It's one and all!' I'd been meaning to hang around near Seth but they yanked me along by the arms and swept me down there. 'One and all!' they kept shouting. 'One and all!' That was for their protection, you understand. They knew damn well what they were doing weren't Federal law. It was mob law they was on, and numbers was their preservation. They didn't mean to let no one stand aside.

They went ranting and raging down to the hanging-tree, which was a big cottonwood with spreading branches, handy for the job. Well, the business didn't take long. The condemned men was asked if they wanted to do any praying, but they turned that down, all three. The ropes was settled round their necks and the horse between the shafts of the cart was give a thwack across the rump that sent him bounding away. The three men spilt off the end of the cart, but as the boards went from under him, I watched Henry Plumer leap high in the air and come down hard on the rope and the knot dig in under his ear and kill him, straight. The other two swung and kicked for a while, but not Henry: his neck was broke at the first drop. He'd made a clean job of his going-out.

'Run 'em up!' came the cry, and the corpses was hauled aloft, and the ropes made fast again, and the three men left hanging high. It was a shocking thing to see how easy life went out of them. There had been so much zing in Henry, and he had done even that last jump with so much fire, and there he was, dangling, fine boots and tail-coat and all. *They* hadn't changed, but as for him that wore them, he was clean gone. They was all three gone, and there weren't no calling them back. Same as when a man gets hit in the right place with a slug of lead. It ain't much of a hole, but see how fast the life leaks out of it. Sights like that make you feel how frail a man's life is: it can be tromped down as easy as a flower. Yet men are so blamed foolhardy with their lives, and go swaggering round the world like they could never die. We all do it, and I suppose there ain't no other way.

The crowd was gathering back at the waggon again. They hadn't forgot Seth. Their blood was up, and it was clear that some of them was looking for more of the same. Mace climbed back on the waggon, and Quarles followed. Mace started in on his speech, saying that as they hadn't caught Seth on the job, if guilt was to be proved, it would have to be by the circumstantial type of evidence. He rambled on a while, trying to drive this point home, but the roughs in the crowd weren't interested in such fancy talking.

'Get on with it!' yells a voice. 'We ain't got all day.'

'Hang him, and be on the safe side!' says another.

'There ain't no call for your circumstantial rubbish,' yells a third. 'We know he was in with Plumer. Ain't that enough to go on?'

'Hold it!' bellows Mace, and he argued with that mob. He said you just couldn't go hanging a feller without proof, but it didn't sound like many of them was won over to that opinion. They kept yelling at him to get on with it, until after a while, Mace was getting desperate. 'Is there anybody here,' he hollers, 'is there anybody that will speak up for this man?' pointing at Seth.

'Yeah,' says I. 'Me. I'll speak.' It fell quiet after that, and I could hear my own voice kind of blundering about in the silence: 'If you ask me, gentlemen, you ain't giving Seth Walsh here a fair shake.'

The troublemakers started jeering again, and before long it had got so bad I could hardly make myself heard.

'Come on, gents,' I yells. 'Let me say my piece. Be fair.'

'Shut your jaw!'

'Hang him with the other,' somebody suggests.

Mr Quarles had seen the fix I was in and now he did his best to help me. He started jumping round on them little legs of his, yelling, 'Ain't a man got a right to a hearing any more?' That slowed the hot-heads down a little, hearing him speak out for me in that way. They hadn't expected moderate counsels from him.

'No, listen,' says I. 'You ain't got a thing on this man. Lord's sakes! because a man's been seen having a drink with Plumer, that don't make him a robber nor a murderer. If it did, there'd be a heap of folks round here in line for the hanging-tree. You've got to be reasonable.'

'Hang 'em both and have done!' yells the same voice, giving his suggestion another airing. It appeared to have gained support in the meantime. Other voices were raised, agreeing with it, and the crowd began to surge forward in a nasty way. I made it clear I was thinking of going for my weapon, and the men in front slowed down, but them behind stayed in favour of rushing me.

There was one hell of a din going on. I could see Mr Quarles hopping up and down on the waggon and yelling, 'Wait a minute. Let's do this right,' but I got the feeling the only person paying attention to his words was me.

Missouri, thinks I to myself, you're in a real jam. One of these toughs is going to sneak around and take you from behind any minute now.

Just at that moment, damn me if I didn't hear a voice, coming from the very direction I was worrying over. 'That'll do!' says the voice, and a shot rang out. I jumped a mile and for a second I was distinctly under the impression that I'd been plugged. Then I realized, and I've never been so glad to recognize that voice, funny accent and all, as I was then. Mr Johnston had arrived.

'Back off,' says Mr Johnston. 'Now, don't aggravate me, gentlemen – I'm asking you in a civil manner to stand back. Anybody that don't comply can expect to have his head blown off.'

The crowd stood back.

'Listen here,' says Mr Johnston. 'This is your court, and I want you to have some respect for it, and not go acting like a passul of savages.'

Folks in the crowd that had thought the same on the quiet

now summoned up pluck to say so out loud, when they was backed by Mr Johnston's gun.

'Anyone that tries to break up this court will have to answer to me,' says Mr Johnston. 'He's only to make himself known by raising hand or voice and I'll give him a fair show, right now.'

There weren't no takers. Mr Johnston hadn't done more than fire in practice since he hit Helena but his reputation had got around somehow.

'Right,' says Mr Johnston. 'Now maybe we can get on with the hearing!'

We did, and it didn't take long for that court to decide that they hadn't no firm evidence against Seth; what they did have didn't come no higher than a vague suspicion, so the Assessors ruled to let him go free. The verdict was put to the vote and passed unanimous, and the crowd drifted away.

'That was a close one!' says Seth as I untied his wrists. 'I figured I was crow-bait there for a while, Missouri. You, too, when you put your word in. Thanks for that.' He was smiling and looking his natural self, save for a twitch that worked every now and then under his left eye. That was the only sign he gave – he had his share of backbone, did Seth!

'Yes sir,' he says, 'I thought I was going to keep old Henry company. Handsome Henry,' says he in a musing voice, staring at the bodies on the tree. 'So long, Henry, old sport.' He shook his head admiringly. 'You know,' he says, 'Henry always did his best to appear smart and elegant, and I'll be damned if he don't look it now, even if he is on the tree.'

We looked for a while at Henry dangling there in his shiny tooled boots and his broidered vest. It was true, he'd seen his time out smart and neat. You had to give him that. Henry was himself to the last breath, even if he was a liar and a murderer.

'Seth,' says I. 'You weren't in with that gang, were you?'

'What, me?' says Seth. 'I knew nothing about it.'

'You're telling me the truth, Seth?'

'Sure,' says he. 'I wouldn't lie to you, Missouri. You got my oath on it. My Bible oath. – And now I figure I'd better go along and thank Mr Johnston.'

'Thank Arthur, too,' says I. 'Thank Arthur when you see him next.'

'Yeah,' says Seth, but he didn't sound too enthusiastic. I guess he didn't like the idea of being beholden in that quarter.

Seth thanked Mr Johnston, and Mr Johnston says, 'Nay, it only makes us square. It makes us even. I don't forget what you boys did for me in Cheyenne.'

We all went for a drink, and it was some time later that, as we rode out of town, we passed the hanging-tree again. The corpses was still there – it was the regular thing to leave them on show till sundown as a general warning to others – they was there, but Henry Plumer's boots had gone. He was dangling there in his socks.

Later, I found out that them boots had found their way into the possession of Mr Quarles. He kept them in that room of his, with the other stuff. He put boot-trees in them, and had them soaped regular, to make sure they stayed in good shape.

5

Belle and Me

There was no Mrs Quarles at this period, so to that extent
the editor has got his facts wrong, but it is true that Belle
laboured to lead me into respectable ways, which proved a
considerable sweat to us both. It was about this time that
Belle began to entertain certain ideas about refinement and
deportment and such matters. Her thoughts was taken up a
good deal by fashionable dresses and fine furniture, and she
got into the way of sending for illustrated catalogues from
some place back East, and spent a heap of time leafing
through them and sighing hard. She used to ask me to sit
beside her, and turn over the pages with her, and give her
my opinions.

Well, I done it. I was mighty fond of Belle at that time,
and would have done most anything for her. She used to
order stuff out of the catalogues, and Mr Quarles encouraged
her, and would even foot the bill. He told me he liked to see
Belle making a lady of herself, and how he needed somebody
with taste and good manners to act as hostess at his dinner-
parties, and Belle was just the ticket for that job. Mr Quarles
had taken to giving these private dinner-parties. He asked all
the top citizens of Helena, and they would come along
without fail, because Mr Quarles was worth a heap of money
by this time, he was bigger than any of them. I reckon them

parties helped prove to Mr Quarles what a top-notcher he was getting to be.

The parties most likely account for the book that Belle bought. It was bound in real hide, and had a fine lady on the cover, stamped in gold, and a golden gentleman a-sweeping off his hat to her. The book was called *Etiquette and Deportment* and for a while it was Belle's Bible. She tormented the life out of me with that book, I know that. She was forever correcting me about my clothes, and the way I said things, and what spoon to pick up when at table.

'I want to improve you,' says Belle. 'I want to make something out of you. Don't stand there grinning, you lunk-head! I mean to make a gentleman out of you.'

Some chance! thinks I, but I will say that Belle persevered. She worked on me, and she worked on herself. She used to act the fine lady at Quarles's dinner-parties, and put on considerable style. But the day came when she turned on that Etiquette book and rent it. She tossed that book around the room and yelled at it, shocking. She says it was so much rubbish, and then she tore the pages out of it and slung them out of the window. I watched page after page go fluttering down on to the heads of the loafers on the board-walk below, and I'll wager that's as near as them boys ever got to Etiquette and Deportment in their entire lives.

The reason why Belle savaged the book was this: She'd been putting on some of her fine airs that she'd learnt from the book, and cutting a dash, as she thought, at one of Quarles's gatherings, when a certain lady had begun to laugh at her, and went on to make fun of her in a sly way, and got other ladies to do the same thing. It weren't kind to laugh and make game of Belle, but when I saw the book go through the window, I could have put that catty lady on a salary. I judged she'd done Belle a service – and I was durn sure she'd done me one.

But if I'd hoped that all the ladylikeness would die down after that, I was soon to find out different. Belle blamed the book for her flop that day, but she still wanted to cut a fine figure. The parties went on, and she used to figure as hostess, and would drag me along to them fairly often. The idea seemed to be that if she exposed me enough times to the top citizens, I'd catch respectability and good manners like a man might catch the smallpox. Quarles didn't mind her bringing me along to his parties; not at all; in fact, he encouraged it. About this time he began to talk of bringing me into the business 'at a more responsible level'. He used to point to me and say: 'There's a keen young feller that could make his mark on business before long. There's a young man with a future,' and the doctor and traders and land-agents gathered round would listen to this rot, and go nodding their heads as if they agreed with it, and had known it all along. Such folks always showed considerable respect for Mr Quarles's opinion now that he'd got so rich.

The first time I was being taken to one of these parties, I remember Belle standing staring at me and shaking her head. 'Look at you,' she says. 'We just got to do something about your clothes, Missouri Fynn!' She done it, too. She rigged me out in a natty black suit, and got me shirts with fancy collars, and had me wearing a watch and chain, and slicked my hair down with bear's grease. When she'd got me all done up like that, she stood back and surveyed her handiwork and says, 'Missouri, I'm going to be proud to be seen in your company. You look uncommon elegant. You've got such fine natural advantages, if only you'll make use of them.' But I didn't like that black suit, and I didn't much care for the dinner-parties, neither. All them business fellers ever talked about was deals and property and what they called 'the good prospects opening up'; or else they huddled round the table when the ladies was out of the way and told jokes that wouldn't have raised a smile in a boy of ten, most of them. I'd sit there in my smart suit, feeling like a hog in an apron. Now and then I'd put in a word, just to appear sociable, but I don't suppose my opinion was worth shucks because I knew nothing about their kind of business. I know I used to come away from Quarles's jollifications feeling pretty low and miserable, and particularly for a young man that had such a fine future ahead of him! I got the impression Belle weren't all that keen on them parties, either, but when I said as much, she got mad. 'Do you want to be nothing all your life?' she says. 'A no-count drifter. Is that what you want? Listen,' she says, 'if you're going to get ahead, you've got to dress smart, and have good manners, and mix with the right people, and be able to talk about deals and mergers, and do your share of smiling, too, not sit there looking like a sick cow. How in the world are you going to work with such high-toned folks as Dr Mace and Mr Farebrother when you don't show an ounce of class yourself? Answer me that!'

'I ain't sure I *want* to work with Dr Mace nor Mr Farebrother, Belle.'

'Aw, come on! Don't be a fool! You want to get ahead, I know you do!' Belle sounded right upset and near to tears, so I didn't say any more. I put up with them parties and done my best to enjoy myself, but it was hard work, and I never did get accustomed to the fancy clothes. If ever Seth saw me wearing them, the most mocking smile would come over his face, and sometimes he'd work his jaw, making remarks about me being done up like the dog's dinner, or looking like a pox-doctor's clerk. You know the sort of thing. I couldn't blame him, in a way.

I got my own back on that suit through croquet. Belle had read in one of her magazines that croquet was all the rage back East, and she persuaded Mr Quarles to have a patch of ground levelled for the sport, and before long, there we was, shuffling round the place, knocking wooden balls through hoops. One time, in bending down to study a shot, I was fortunate enough to rip my suit right across the shoulders. The suit was ruined, but as things turned out, that didn't help me. Belle insisted on picking me out another suit, even fancier than the last, and there had to be new lace-fronted shirts to go with it, and I don't know what else, until I was begging her to stop.

It struck me as strange that Seth and Belle never gave each other so much as a 'Good day' any more. She'd turned against him, ever since Henry Plumer was brought to trial and hanged. He seemed to have gone against her, too, and if she came into the saloon when he was there, he'd turn his back on her and generally give her the cold shake. Seth was still friendly with Lily, though. Poor Lily, she went right down for a while after Plumer's death, but then her spirits rose again, and they kept on rising till they was on the boil. Maybe Plumer's hanging marked Lily, I don't know; but it's certain that she grew more reckless afterwards, and used to say she was out for a good time while she could, and be damned to the rest of it. She'd tackle her bottle like a man, sometimes, and raise hell with the boys, and then her pretty face got more red and her dark eyes grew bigger and more staring. She just didn't give a cuss. Mr Quarles never interfered with Lily no more. She was mighty popular with the customers, so Quarles threw the rule-book away so far as Lily was concerned, and let her do more or less as she pleased, and gave all his attention to Belle.

Lily was never asked to Quarles's dinner-parties: she'd be in the bar, whooping it up with the boys. Sometimes, just for fun, she'd dress up in men's duds, and then she would strut around in a slouch hat, a studded leather vest and boots with Spanish spurs. She even wore a gun-belt and made out like she was a gunfighter. There was a song she used to sing on that subject that was a mighty sassy number and a prime favourite with the customers at the Eagle. It was all made up from gunhands' talk, and I can still remember it. Lily used to climb up on a table to sing it, and while she was performing she'd do some pretty outrageous things with the Colt she'd have drawn from her holster. This is how the song went, and the joke lies in the double meanings:

> I met a feller
> Yesterday.
> We had a fuss,
> He made his play.
> What in the world is a girl to do,
> When a feller gets the bulge on you?
>
> Another feller,
> Thrown down on me,
> A mean gunslinger,
> Right *horn*ery.
> What in the world is a girl to do,
> When a feller gets the drop on you?
>
> He called me out,
> And then he drew.

This girl was plugged:
He blowed me through.
What in the world is a girl to do,
When a shooter lies over you?

Maybe you can see what I mean. Folks used to say that Lily
was getting worse than any crib-girl in the way she behaved,
and in a way that was true, because a crib-girl has to be
discreet and keep to her employment, whereas young Lily
did as she pleased, and gave away what a crib-girl sells, if she
felt so inclined, but at other times she'd scorn men, and drive
them away, and laugh at them for fools and sots.

Belle told me she didn't want to have to do with men like
Seth no more. That was all right by me, because Seth was a
hard man to have against you when it come to the ladies.
But not content with that, Belle started saying that *I*
oughtn't to go wasting my time with him, either. I reminded
her that Seth was still a partner of mine, and anyway, what
was wrong with me seeing him. I told her she was acting like
she was scared of Seth.

'Scared of him?' she says. 'That's a good one!' Then she
says, 'It's not just Seth – though he's the worst. There's
others you hang around with.'

'Such as who?'

'Oh, I don't know,' she says. 'Deadbeats like Johnston and
that young breed. Arthur.'

'What's wrong with them?'

'They're weird. They're a weird bunch. They're not the
kind for you.'

'A sight less weird than fellers like Mace and Farebrother.'

'They're no-hopers, that's what. As for Mace and

Farebrother, that's a different matter.' Belle had the grace to give a smile. 'Maybe they're weird, too, in a different way, but you *got* to team up with people like that.'

'Not me, I don't.'

'All right then,' says she with a shrug. '*Be* skin-poor all your days!'

'I ain't skin-poor now,' says I, but Belle had gone swirling away, riding on her high horse. She didn't like to be contradicted on that subject.

Maybe I've been giving a wrong impression of Belle just lately, because although she did have this bee in her bonnet about improving herself, and improving me, too, most of the time she was still the same sweet woman, and so handsome. She was a favourite at the Eagle, too, but men gave her more respect than they did to Lily. For instance, I heard a feller say one night, 'I'd like the dark-haired one to be my tart, but the blonde one to be my bride.' His friend glanced across in my direction and says, 'You're wasting your time even thinking about that.'

It was his words that put the idea into my head. Suddenly, it was clear to me that one day Belle would just naturally up and marry somebody. It stood to reason. My heart came up into my mouth at the idea, and I figured that the somebody had better be me. I went out to one side for a couple of days to think about the situation, and then I buzzed along to see Belle. The only trouble with my scheme was that she probably wouldn't have me, not unless I agreed to a lifetime of Mace and Farebrother, and talking deals round dinner-tables.

I found her at her dressing-table, doing her hair.

'Belle,' says I. 'You've got to listen. I've had a great idea.'

'That's not like you, Missouri.' I could hear she was in one of her sassy moods. 'You want to be careful. Well,' she says, 'what is your great idea, hon?'

'You and me, Belle.'

'What about us?'

'How if we got married?'

She sat stock still, one hand in the air, holding up the hairbrush. Then she turned round slow and gave me a sort of wondering smile.

'Aw!' she says in a soft voice and started shaking her head. 'Is that your great idea?'

'Right!' says I, feeling encouraged. 'How about it, Belle?'

'If you ain't the sweetest boy,' she murmurs.

I judged I was getting along fine. It was turning out to be a sight easier than I'd expected.

'You're a young lunkhead, but I love you for it. I'm right touched,' says she.

'Great!' says I. 'When we going to do it? Tomorrow? No sense in hanging around.'

'Tomorrow? Oh sure! – Wait, I've got an even better idea. Why don't we run and find a preacher right now?'

'I'm game,' says I. 'Get your hat, Belle.'

'You would, too!' she says, laughing. 'You young mad-head!'

'Let's go, Belle. Let's go!'

'Wait a minute,' says Belle, putting on a serious face. 'May I ask you, Mr Fynn, where you intend to accommodate your lucky bride?'

'I'll find a place, Belle.'

'Like that shack on your claim, maybe? We could always share it with Mr Johnston and the others, huh?'

'No,' says I. 'No, I don't think that would quite answer. But I'll find somewhere, Belle, never fear.'

'I can't help feeling a little nervous.'

'Don't bother your head about it, honey.'

'My Saviour!' says she. 'I almost *could* do it, to hear you talk!'

'Sure you could. Let's go.'

'Not a chance!' she raps out. 'I ain't marrying you.'

I flopped down into a chair, feeling like I'd taken a punch in the wind, a solid one.

'Why not?' says I, in a creaky voice.

'There's lots of reasons – but most of all I just ain't ambitious to live in a cabin and be poor. I'm not going to be a housewife, Missouri, it just ain't my style. I'm not going to work my fingers to the bone for nobody, not even you.' Then she softened. 'Listen,' she says. 'It's not that I don't like you, Missouri. I do. I like you a lot.'

'Well then . . . ?'

'Have you been listening? Have you taken in a word I said? Oh, Missouri,' says she, shaking her head. 'What *am* I going to do with you?'

'Marry me would be best.'

'There you go again! Can't you understand? You stubborn mule! Listen. Get this through your thick skull. Are you listening?'

'Yes, Belle.'

'It's *money* makes this mare go! What do you say to that?'

'What do I say? I say it ain't true. I know you, Belle, and I know what you said ain't more than a mean sort of bragging. That ain't the real Belle talking.'

'Yes it is,' she says, awful fierce. 'It *is*, it *is*, it *is*! That's really me. So think on that!'

I went away after that. She'd convinced me. I did think on

her words, too, over the coming days and weeks, and I recalled how often she'd told me I ought to try to get ahead and be somebody. I reckon it was the memory of that pushed me into closing with Mr Quarles when he come to me with his offer.

6

Mr Quarles proposed a business partnership to Fynn, which could have been the making of him. . . .

On the Shares with George Quarles

Mr Quarles raised his proposition in this way:

'Ever heard of a feller by the name of Storey?' he asks. He'd got me into his office to ask this question in private; it was the same place where I'd seen him being dragged round on the end of a halter by that crib-girl, Marlene, but you'd never have guessed he indulged in such antics to look at him now. He looked 'the astute and upright man of business' all right, rubbing his hands and stroking his whiskers, his eyes as bright as a ferret's, and his manner as friendly as could be.

'Nope,' says I. 'Who's Storey?'

'From up Alder Gulch way. A miner.'

'Did he strike it rich, or something?'

'Did he strike it rich?' Mr Quarles gave a jovial laugh. 'You could say so, Missouri. But his gold walked on four legs.'

'Sounds like a riddle, Mr Quarles.'

'Call me George,' says he. 'I think we know each other well enough by now.'

I figured by that something must be in the air, to make Quarles so durn generous with his given name, all of a sudden.

'Storey took fifteen thousand dollars down into Texas. Right?' says he. 'With that sum of money he purchased for himself a good herd of longhorns and drove them back up here, which was a smart move.'

'Now I remember,' says I.

'It would be an even smarter move if somebody was to do it again now. You know why? The railroads are scheduled to come this way before long. Right? This time it wouldn't just be supplying beef to the mining-camps, like Storey did; this time it would be shipping cattle back East along the line of rail. That means real big business. It means bonanza.' He waited a minute for his words to sink in, then he says, 'How does that sound to you, Missouri?'

'How does what sound to me?'

'The cattle business, what else? How about if you was to go down there and bring back a herd of longhorns, like Storey did?'

'That sounds like a considerable sweat.'

'Would you do it, Missouri?'

'There's two things you got wrong, Mr Quarles . . .'

'– George,' says he. 'Call me George.'

'Yeah, well, there's two things you got wrong. First, I ain't got the necessary . . .'

'No,' says he, 'but that's my part. I've got the money, and I've got the land. We go into this on the shares, Missouri.'

'Second, I ain't no cowpuncher . . .'

He waved this away as if it weren't worth shucks. 'That don't matter,' says he. 'You can hire yourself drovers down there. It's not a problem, getting cowhands. My difficulty is in finding a man I can trust to put in charge. A man who can boss the drive. A man who can back up his words, if necessary.' He tapped his right side where his hand-gun

82

would have been, if he ever carried a weapon, which he never did. 'I thought of you as the man in charge. What do you say?'

For a while, I didn't say nothing. I was turning the proposal round in my head.

'It'll take you maybe five months, Missouri,' says he. 'Five little months and then, if all goes well, you'll find yourself rich. You'll be a made man!'

I got to thinking about Belle, and what she'd said to me. If you looked at it like that, Quarles's offer come near to being providential, and I figured I'd just *have* to take on. Besides, if I turned the offer down and word of me doing that ever reached Belle's ears, she'd look on me as a real no-hoper and write me off for certain.

Quarles was still talking. 'It would be a partnership,' he was saying. 'That's the point to keep in mind. A partnership. When you got back, you could either stay on the shares with me – which is what I hope – or else you could take your cut and set up as a ranch-man on your own. But, either way, you'll be in for a quarter share of the cattle.'

I couldn't help but give a whistle. 'A quarter share,' says I. 'That's mighty generous – George.'

'It'll be worth it, all round,' says he. 'You mark my words. You'll agree then?'

I nodded. 'OK.'

'Great!' says he, all smiles. 'Strike hands on a bargain,' and shoves out his hand to shake. I took it in mine and it was soft and clammy, and I was set up in a business partnership.

I'd hoped I might take some company down to Texas with me, but neither Seth nor Mr Johnston was keen on going. Mr Johnston just shook his head and says he was getting too old for such trips, his bones ached in his hip, and he didn't figure he'd be much help to me. It would be better, says he, if he stayed put and kept an eye on the claim. Mr Johnston was very quiet these days and didn't stir much from the shack, so I weren't too surprised to find he weren't going. I thought Seth might have, but he laughed at the idea. He says he ain't no cowhand, and he don't mean to spend the next few months eating dust behind a crowd of bony-arsed critturs. 'Besides,' says Seth, 'it wouldn't seem natural to have you for a boss. Seth Walsh ain't about to take orders from the Missouri Kid.'

'It wouldn't be like that,' says I.

Seth just laughs and says, 'Go ahead and do it if you want to, cowpoke, but you can count me out. I got other business to attend to.'

So I said goodbye to Mr Johnston and Seth and Lily and Arthur and all the folks I knew, and the day before I hit the trail for Texas, Mr Quarles threw me a little celebration. There was just Belle and Quarles and me, and we drank to success, and I called him 'George', and Belle smiled so sweet on both of us, and when I came to leave, I surprised a tear shining in Belle's eye, which cheered me up because it showed she was going to miss me.

It was spring when I lit out for Texas, with my gun at my hip and a new repeater rifle in my saddle-holster which Mr Quarles had given me as a farewell present – the rifle, I mean. Now, I ain't going to tell you all that happened on the cattle-drive. Just take it from me that it was hard slog for months together, but we had good luck and brought the herd safe back to Montana, me and the Texan cowpunchers I'd hired. Them Texans was first-class men, I will say; they was real hard-twisted riders that did their job in a Number

One style. We made good time, and one reason was that the men wanted to be on the back-trail to Texas before the hard weather set in.

It was spring when I set out, and it was fall by the time I got back within striking distance of Helena. Once there, I left my men guarding the herd a few miles out of town and rode in to report to Mr Quarles, straight off – or that's who I told myself I was hurrying to see.

Helena sure looked good after those months on the plains. She even smelt good: there was the sweet smell of baking bread wafting in the air of her streets, and the scent of men and horses crowded together, sweat and hay and trampled droppings, and the sharp tang of woodsmoke from the stoves. So many lights was burning in the dusk, and music was sounding from the saloons, loud and jolly. I thought I'd never seen so many folks; they was swarming all over the place, and there was a feeling of excitement about the whole thing, like you get sometimes in towns, and particularly when the twilight is coming down.

I pushed straight on to the Eagle but I couldn't raise Quarles, nor Belle neither. All I could do was to settle down and wait for them to put in an appearance. The place was jam-full and I had middling difficulty getting up to the bar. I made my order, but when I shoved the money for the drink over to the barman, he shoved it back at me, yelling over the din, 'On the house, tonight, friend!'

No wonder the barman was sweating! On the house? thinks I. What's got into Mr Quarles? That ain't his usual style.

It weren't long before I saw Seth come shouldering his way through the bar. I could tell at a glance that he was mellow: his brown eyes was shiny with liquor.

'Well,' says he, ranging up on me, 'look'ee here! If it ain't the wanderer returned! How's it going, Missouri? You got corns on your ass?'

'It's going fine,' says I. 'Hey, where is everybody?'

'Going fine, huh? You just hit town?'

'That's right, Seth.'

'I don't suppose you been back to the cabin nor nothing?'

'I rode straight here to see Quarles.'

'Uh-uh. And you got that herd back safe for him, did you?'

'Sure did.'

'Well now,' says he, fixing me with one of his strange smiles. 'Pretty going-on, one way and another.'

Seth signalled over the counter, and the barman gave him a drink, right smart.

'Is he around?' says I.

'Is who around?' says Seth, jerking his head up from the glass.

'Quarles, of course. I can't seem to raise him.'

'Ah yes.' Seth gave me a long, thoughtful, muzzy look.

'Let's go outside, partner,' says he. 'I want a private word with you.'

I followed him into the street. As he stood there, hesitating and searching for words, a crowd of men came surging round the corner and swept on towards us. They was in great spirits, capering and yelling and loosing off guns; some had pans and they was banging on them with sticks; some was leaping in the air and cracking their heels together and crying, 'Whoo-oop!'; and all in all, they was raising a rare old din.

'Come on,' says Seth. 'We're joining the party,' and took me by the arm and dragged me into the crowd. We was swept along with the others, and had bottles shoved at us, and pistols let off by our ears, and pans clattering round us in a wild ra-ta-tan.

'What's the idea?' I yells, but Seth took no notice and I figured he couldn't hear me in the racket.

The crowd come to a halt outside Rapson's Hotel, and we was all milling round there. By that time, they was giving the following chant:

> Lucky man.
> Lucky man.
> Show yourself,
> If you can.

When I heard that, I had it figured for a charivari. In case you don't know what a charivari is, I'll tell you: a charivari is a kind of spree that follows on a wedding out West. The first night the happy couple are spliced, the boys all get liquored up and they march to the place them newly-weds is staying and kick up hell outside the bedroom window. Such things are considered to be fun by lots of folks.

Next, the crowd started on another chant, and it was:

> Blushing bride,
> Don't you hide.

> Blushing bride,
> Come outside.

A light came on in the upstairs window of Rapson's, and a minute or two later, the door on to the balcony opened. When I saw who came through that door, my heart all but stopped and my legs grew weak. First there came Mr Quarles, grinning, and waving down at the crowd, and after him there came Belle, looking mighty handsome in a white gown, with her gold hair loose and streaming across her shoulders, and she was smiling, too. She put one hand on Quarles's arm and gave a wave with the other, and the crowd sent up a monstrous cheer. I looked at the couple, and Belle was half a head taller than Quarles.

To see them there like that – well, it gave me the most solid punch I ever took in my entire life. I was reeling. My brain couldn't believe it, and yet I knew it were so. It was no dream. The noise of the crowd went roaring in my ears, and for a few seconds it was almost like I was uprooted and blown away by it, like a tree in a gale. Then I got myself together, but I still felt cut down and desperate, with no help anywhere in sight.

Quarles was talking by now. 'My friends,' he yells. 'Thanks, one and all, for giving us such a good send-off. Believe me, we really do appreciate your gesture. But now –' wagging a coy finger at them – 'now the time has come for us to settle down to a good night's sleep. I'm sure you'll understand.'

As he said this, Quarles simpered like a riven dish and hugged Belle round the waist. You can imagine how the crowd hooted and cheered and stamped their feet at his words, but I could recall Quarles in the bloody shirt, and the crib-girl Marlene, and the noose and all, and his words burnt on me like a smoking brand. I gave a growl and spun away down the street, running like a crazy man.

Next thing I knew I was standing up at a bar in some two-bit saloon with a bottle in front of me, and I couldn't remember either coming into that bar nor ordering that bottle; all I did know was that I was tackling the bottle like fury. Then I saw Seth standing alongside me. He didn't say nothing, he just stood there, like he was waiting.

I turned on him: 'Why didn't you tell me, Seth?' I bawls. 'You should have told me!'

He just spread out his hands and says, 'I didn't know how.'

That stopped me. I nodded. I could see what he meant: it was well nigh untellable.

'Stay and drink with me, anyhow,' says I. 'Do that much for me, Seth.'

'Sure,' says he, and he did.

I got rotten drunk that night, but I judge I had provocation enough to excuse a saint. The idea of that bedroom in Rapson's Hotel would keep sidling into my mind, and I'd drink some more to be rid of it. The last thing I remember was asking Seth: 'How could she do it? With him! How could she bring herself?' Seth gave a shrug and says, 'It looks like Quarles can buy up just about anything he has a mind to.'

Soon after that, I blacked out, and Seth loaded me on my horse and led me back to our cabin on the claim outside town.

7

Mr Quarles proposed a business partnership to Fynn which could have been the making of him, but Fynn chose to throw away this opportunity. . . .

Why I Turned it in with Quarles

I opened my eyes next morning, not knowing where I was. All I did know was that I felt horrible rusty. Then there was this other feeling, like I'd lost something important but couldn't figure out what. A feller once told me how he was hit by a locomotive and when he woke up in bed later, he just *knew* that a dreadful thing had happened to him but he couldn't work out what it was. Then he tried to get out of bed and found one of his legs had gone. It was rather that way with me. First, I didn't remember, but then I saw Seth up and already moving round the cabin, and at the sight of him I did remember, and it was like the moment when the feller tried to get out of bed: I remembered why I felt so bad and how I came to be there, and I groaned.

Seth came over to bring me some coffee, and I saw he was dressed, ready for the trail.

'Thanks,' I says. 'You going out?'

'A little private business to attend to.'

I sat up and drank the coffee, and it struck me there was something about the shack that weren't as it should be. 'Hey,' says I. 'Where's Mr Johnston?'

'Gone,' says he.

'Gone?'

'I told you last night. Don't you remember, Missouri? We had quite a conversation about it.'

I shook my head. 'Gone?'

'That's right. Packed his traps and blown. I told you.'

'Mr Johnston gone? Didn't he leave no word for me? No message?'

'He just says, "Tell Missouri I'm moving on."'

'That's downright amazing.'

'Is it?' says Seth, with a slow smile. 'You know he always was the queerest feller.'

'Yeah but...'

'Well, there it is. I've got to go now, partner.'

'Shall I see you?' I was beginning to feel pretty lonely, I guess.

'I'll be back, later,' says Seth. 'It ain't none of my business, Missouri, but didn't you ought to do something about that herd?'

'Yeah,' says I. The truth was, I'd clean forgot about it, with all my other trouble. But then I thought of them cowhands and how they wanted to take the back-trail down to Texas, and what good men they'd been for me, and I knew I should have to go and report to Quarles right off, for their sake. I dragged myself up and dressed and took the road for Helena, but my heart was heavy at the prospect.

I went in at the side-door of the Eagle and was just climbing the stairs to the office when a well-known voice calls, 'Missouri.'

I stopped in my tracks. I looked, and saw it was Belle, peeping round the edge of a door.

'Can I talk to you?' she says, murmuring soft as a dove.

I didn't say nothing. I stood there, my head swarming with fantastic notions.

'Come on, Missouri.'

Well, I went. I stalked into that hotel bedroom and let her close the door behind me.

'Hello, Missouri, honey,' says she in a dreamy voice.

I found it hard to talk. My windpipe seemed all knotted up. 'How did you know to look for me?' I was croaking like a frog.

'Oh, I got word you were back.' She looked at me with big wide blue eyes. 'You aren't mad at me, are you, Missouri?'

'It's just . . . I can't figure it. You and Quarles. It makes no sense.'

'No sense?' she murmurs. 'I'm his wife, Missouri.'

'Well, I know that.'

'His *legal* wife. Don't you understand. Lord's sakes, Missouri, you didn't expect me to turn that opportunity down?'

'You turned me down,' I croaks.

'George ain't a bad sort,' she says quickly. 'A girl could do worse than George – but I don't want my Missouri to be mad at me. I want him to understand.'

I saw she was aiming to pet and cajole me, like I was a child to be talked out of a bad mood. My voice loosened up when I realized that. 'Understand?' I says. 'Yeah, I reckon I do understand now. You got all that you want, ain't you, Belle? Silk dresses and all such fol-de-rols; smart carriages to do your jaunting in; tony dinner-parties with Dr Mace and Mr Farebrother and all that high-class bunch; everything your heart desires.'

'Not quite,' says she. 'There's one thing missing.'

We stood there, staring hard at each other.

'Listen, Missouri,' she says. 'In a way, you could say I did it for you, too.'

'That's rot!'

'Yes, I did. And anyway, it needn't make so much difference, Missouri, not between you and me. We can still be . . . friends and all. There are ways I can help you now, Missouri, and I aim to do that.'

'Well,' says I, 'seems like that about wraps it up. It's funny, you know, but the only way I could figure things was that Quarles must have forced you, somehow.'

'Forced me?' She gave a brassy laugh. 'Show some sense! Anyway,' she goes on, '*you* know that what happened between me and George last night weren't happening for the first time. Not by a long way. The only difference was, I'd got my legal rights last night.'

I stood there a long time, letting that speech sink in. Then I says, 'There's one other difference: I never knew before.'

'How do you mean?'

'I never knew about you and Quarles.'

She flushed right up her neck. Then she yelled at me: 'You must have done. Everybody knew. You're just trying to be ornery.'

'It looks like everybody knew but me. I never knew.'

Belle looked at me, her hand up to her mouth. 'Oh God!' she says. 'Oh sweetheart. *That's* why you're so sore. You never knew! You never guessed!' She was sort of sobbing and laughing at the same time. 'Lord's sakes, if you aren't the world's biggest innocent! Oh, Missouri, what are we going to do with you?' and she put up a hand to stroke my face, but I sheered away. I didn't want her to touch me then.

93

I saw the way it was now, saw it plain. Belle wanted Quarles and his money, wanted him tied fast and sure, but she wanted to keep up her claim on me, too. She thought I'd settle for that! Once I understood, I felt empty and numb and kind of lightheaded, so I sat down in a chair.

Belle was still talking but I weren't listening no more. By and by, she gave up and just stood there, her hands on her hips and her chest heaving, and she did look awful pretty, there was no denying it. 'Can't you say something, Missouri?' she pleads. 'You act like you've been struck dumb.'

'I guess I'm all out of talk,' says I, and as I spoke, I pushed up on to my feet. Belle flinched away, and I saw she was scared of me for all her bold manner.

'Hell!' says I. 'You don't think I'd hurt you? You got me wrong, Belle,' and I walked to the door.

'Wait!' she calls. 'Where are you going, Missouri?'

'I'm going to see that new husband of yours,' says I. 'But don't worry, I ain't going to hurt him, either.'

She called out after me another couple of times, but I went, anyway.

Mr Quarles was in his office, and was he full of himself! It must have looked to him like everything was coming good at once and he was simply bubbling over with high spirits. He praised me considerable for bringing that herd up safe, and never seemed to notice that I weren't doing much answering. Then he sits back and says, 'You know the latest with me, Missouri? I'm spliced at last.'

'So I heard.'

'Yes sir! I never thought I'd do it, but I've gone and done it. The way I see it, Belle will be a real help to me in all sorts of ways, and particularly when we get to Chicago.'

'Chicago, did you say?'

'That's right. Ah, but of course, you don't know. We plan to make our home in Chicago before long, Belle and me. We're going up there on a sort of honeymoon visit to look for a suitable property, and I expect that by the end of the year . . . Well, my interests there are growing and I've got to be around to look after them. That means I look to you in Montana, partner.'

'To me?'

'Sure. I need somebody to keep an eye on things at this end, the cattle business in particular, and the man of my choice is you, Missouri.'

'No, thanks,' says I. 'Not me. I don't want it.'

'You mean you're going to take your share out?' He sounded real disappointed.

'That's right. But I don't want the cattle. You can buy them back off me.'

'Has something gone wrong?' he asks. 'Has anybody crossed you? You know, Missouri, I'd dearly like for to have you working with me – as a partner.'

'Just name me a price, and get it over.'

'Well,' says he, and I knew that sly thoughts were taking over in his brain. 'Let's see.' He done a few calculations on a piece of paper and then came up with a miserable price – I guess he just couldn't help it, the old sharp.

'All right,' says I, and took his offer without argument which seemed to offend him.

Once that was settled, I didn't hang around. I was just on my way to the door when I remembered to ask: 'Is Arthur still at the Eagle?'

'Who?' says Quarles. 'Oh, you mean the breed.' He started in to laugh. 'If you ain't the strangest feller!' he says, between chuckles. 'You just turn down a big proposition from me and in the next breath, you're enquiring after a young breed. You got me foxed, Missouri.'

'Well? Is he around?'

'Yeah, he's around, as of now. But not for much longer.'

'How's that?'

'Well, there've been complaints. He's growing bigger, and he's been *looking* at folks.'

'Looking at folks?'

'Yeah. The kitchen women, and they don't like it. Nobody's going to stand that from a breed, now are they? So it looks like Arthur will have to go. Why did you want to see him anyway?'

'Let's say I just wanted to exchange a word with somebody honest in this town,' says I, and left him there behind his desk, stroking his whiskers and shaking his head.

8

... Fynn chose to throw away this opportunity and return to his aimless, drifting life, alone this time, after his quarrel with Seth Walsh and the disappearance of Mr Johnston.

'So Long, Saphead'

Arthur was in the back place, washing dirty crocks. I stood in the doorway and watched him wiping out dirty plates with his finger and then putting the finger in his mouth. When he saw me, he acted awful strange. His face started working, and he looked like he wouldn't have minded slinking out of the way, if only he could have got to a door, which he couldn't, being as I was standing in the only one.

'Hi, Arthur,' says I, holding out my hand. 'Great to see you again. Have you missed me at all?'

Instead of shaking my hand, he backed away and flattened against the wall, his eyes bugging right out. 'It weren't my fault,' he whines.

'What's wrong, Arthur? What the hell's wrong?' It seemed as if the whole world had gone crazy since I'd been down to Texas. I walked over to Arthur, and damn me if the boy didn't cower down and huddle in the corner, like he was shrinking from me. He was muttering like fury now, and in among the gibberish, I heard him say the name of Mr Johnston more than once.

'Tell me what's amiss, Arthur,' says I, hauling him to

his feet. 'Did Mr Johnston hurt you in some way. Is that it?'

'I . . . scared.'

'I can see that, Arthur. But why? Did you have some sort of trouble with Mr Johnston?'

The boy didn't answer. He was trembling all over, like a nervous animal.

'Because if you did,' I says, 'you can relax. You hear? You don't have to worry no more: Mr Johnston's left town.'

The only reply Arthur gave me was a moan.

'You hear? He's gone.'

'It weren't my fault, Missouri.'

'Well then, if it weren't your fault, what are you so scared about?'

'I'm scared,' he mumbles, rolling his eyes. 'I'm scared of Mr Johnston's ghost.'

That stopped me in my tracks for a minute. Then I thinks, poor boy, he's flipped. 'What are you talking about, Arthur?' says I. 'Mr Johnston ain't dead. How can he have a ghost if he ain't dead?'

'Yes,' says he. 'Dead. Mr Johnston dead.'

'You mean he's *dead*?'

Arthur was sobbing. 'I seen it,' he says, 'but I never told nobody because I daren't. That's why he'll come and haunt me. For revenge.'

'You're joking!' says I, though it was clear the boy was in a state of downright terror. 'Tell me what happened? What did you see?'

'Please, Missouri, no. Don't make me.'

'Listen,' says I. 'You tell me and I'll arrange it so his ghost stays clear of you. Otherwise . . .' I gave a shrug.

He was quiet for a while, thinking about my offer. Then he says, 'Promise?'

'Sure. You got my word.'

He thinks some more and then finally he whispers, 'Seth put him in water.'

'Seth *what*?'

'He tied a big stone to Mr Johnston and then he sunk him in the creek.'

I felt the hair go crawling on my head. 'You mean – Seth drownded him?' I was whispering too, now.

'No. Not drownded. He was shot dead. Two times ...' The boy pointed to his chest. 'Here.'

'Oh my God! You aren't telling me that Seth ... ?'

Arthur just stared at me.

'You've got to take me there,' says I. 'You've got to show me the place where Mr Johnston's lying.'

'N-o-o,' wails Arthur, and slumped down on the floor again.

'Sorry, Arthur,' says I, sounding grim, 'but you've just got to take me there. With a thing as important as this ...'

'I can't. I can't.'

'If not,' says I, 'my promise don't hold. My promise about the ghost. So come on!' and I yanked him back on his feet. I meant to force him into it.

Poor boy, he did take me, though he was monstrous scared and blubbered most of the way. He led me to a place about a mile upstream from our cabin, a place where the river swung in a bend and had scoured out a deep pool below an overhang of rock. It was an awful dark and murky pool, and I couldn't help thinking that if a man *should* be anxious to dump a corpse, this was a fitting place for the job. Weight your dead man so he lay stark on the bottom and leave him for the fish to nibble; put him there early in the year and the spring rise would bring down mud enough to cover what was left of him and plant his bones where no man could stumble on them and no dog grub them up. I stared a long time into that sulky water, and might have made a dive if only I could swim, and I asks myself, Is Mr Johnston really down there? Just then a fish ringed the surface of the pool, and I couldn't help but shudder. It was like he'd sent me his answer.

Arthur was tugging at my sleeve so I let him lead me. He took me over to the right, and pointed to a place at the foot of a big tree. 'You dig,' he says. 'Dig there. You see.' I hadn't a spade but I was wearing my knife so I used that. I sweated away for a while but I didn't come up with nothing but pebbles and dirt, and I began to wonder if maybe Arthur weren't making the whole thing up; after all, I'd got nothing but his word to go on.

Then my knife-blade struck leather, and I hefted out a tattered wallet with his full name stamped on it: *Adolphus Johnston*. He'd never let nobody into the secret of his given name while he lived, and now I saw why. It was the sort of name that could only lead a man into trouble. Then the reality of what I'd found came over me. It's true, thinks I, in a panic sweat. It's true! He's lying in that pool. Oh God, it's true!

Next, my knife fetched up a locket with a wisp of brown hair in it, and on the frame was engraved the name of 'Mary'. I knew he kept the locket in memory of his dead wife that lay buried down in Denver. I didn't dig no more. What was the use? I'd got enough. I stood up and put the locket in my breeches pocket. I knew why Seth had buried such stuff as the wallet and the locket. They was light articles such as might have been swept down by the current, and gone aground on some sandbank further down stream, and led to awkward questions. Mr Johnston's in that pool for sure, thinks I. He's down there in the dimness, on that muddy bed, with the silt falling like snow, and the fishes picking at his bones. He'd come a long way and followed a mournful trail, right back from Sheffield, and when he finished up here, it was like a drowned dog.

I knew what I had to do. I told Arthur to go back to town and watched him spin away like the devil was at his heels. Then I rode to the claim to have it out with Seth.

He was there, lounging in the sun, his back against the cabin wall, his hat down over his eyes, and his legs sprawled out in front of him.

'Bet you don't know who I've just seen,' says I.

'Nope.' He sounded drowsy with the sun.

'I was in town, and I run into somebody I didn't expect. You listening to me, Seth?'

'Mmm. Sure. You ran into somebody.'

'I ran into Mr Johnston.'

Seth sat bolt upright and pushed the hat off his eyes. 'Rubbish,' he says. 'You can't have.' He tried to sound casual but the colour drained from his face and I thought I'd never seen a man look more guilty.

'Why can't I, Seth?'

'Because he's gone, that's why.'

'He's come back.'

'No he ain't!' Seth's voice sounded shrill.

'I tell you he's in town. What's more, he's fixing to come over and pay us a visit.'

'You're a liar,' rasps Seth. Then he struggled to get hold of himself and even raised a hollow laugh. 'What kind of game are you playing, Missouri?' says he.

'No game. I just left him. And look what he sent you.'

I tossed the locket into Seth's lap. 'He told me to say he'd be calling on you soon.'

Seth jumped to his feet like he'd been stung. The locket fell on the ground and lay there winking in the sun, with Seth staring at it like a mesmerized man. 'Where'd you get this?' he mumbles, at last.

'Killed him, didn't you?' says I. 'Shot him down and sunk him in the pool. You snake!'

Seth stared at me. His face was blank, and I guess he was bewildered by my sudden switch.

'What you want to go and do a low-down trick like that for, Seth?'

He kept on staring at me, and by God, if a smile didn't come creeping over his face.

'You smirk at me,' says I, 'and I'll blow you through, the way I feel right now. Wipe it off, or as God's my judge, I'll plug you!'

'What?' says he. 'You mean you'd shoot me?'

'You heard what I said.'

'I ain't heeled, Missouri,' says he in his mildest voice. 'I'm not wearing my irons, if you'll notice.'

'I can still do it.'

'You mean you'd blow me through and give me no show at all? Could you do a thing like that, Missouri?'

'How much of a show did you give Mr Johnston?' says I. 'I'll tell you how much! You gave him none! You must have sneaked up and taken him unawares.'

'That's a lie!'

'You must have sneaked up. Did you plug him from behind? Yeah, I guess that was it.'

'You're wrong, Missouri.'

'Because, if you'd faced him, you'd never have stood a chance.'

'I'm faster than you give me credit for.'

'You mean you got the bulge on Mr Johnston. Don't make me laugh. Why, you cheap skate...'

'Listen here to me, Missouri.'

'... you'd never have come near him. We both know that.'

'Will you *listen*!' he yells, and I saw the twitch had started up under his left eye. 'Will you shut your mouth for a minute and let me speak.'

'I'm inclined to shut your mouth for good,' says I, but I let him talk.

'Once you'd gone on your blamed Texas trip,' says Seth, 'Mr Johnston got a sight worse. You remember how he could be, muttering round the place or else not saying a word, well, he got worse. In fact, he got like he was more than half crazy. One night he picked a quarrel with me, right here in the shack. Picked it deliberate, he did. Naturally, I didn't want no fuss with a man of Johnston's reputation, but he pushed me and pushed me till I couldn't back down. Then he called me out and went for his weapon. I did my best to defend myself – there ain't a feller breathing would have done any different – but I judged it was goodbye for me, all the same. I was the most astonished man in the world when he went down to my gun. I couldn't hardly believe it, though I was seeing it with my own eyes: There he was, dead on the floor, and there I was, still on my two feet. It was only afterwards I understood why. When I picked up his guns off the floor, do you know what? – They weren't loaded! He must have emptied the chambers *before* he picked his quarrel, so he *must* have been crazy. He chose to fight me with empty guns, like he meant me to kill him. Can you believe that? – I know it's hard to take.'

'I ain't sure,' says I. I thought to myself: It could have been like that. It was possible that Mr Johnston had sought out the Blood Atonement he was waiting for, but on the other hand, Seth knew about the Atonement and was capable of making up just such a story to fool me and cover himself. 'I wished I could have seen them guns, that's all,' says I.

'You got my oath that I'm telling the truth,' says Seth.

'Yeah, your oath, but I've met that article once too often.'

'You calling me a liar?' says he, sneering a little.

'If it happened like you say, why didn't you report it, Seth? Why didn't you tell the Marshal? Why did you stow Mr Johnston away in secret and bury his things?'

'How do you know I did?'

'You sunk him in that pool, Seth, with a stone to weight him. You put him under like a stray dog. After he'd saved your life, too!'

'Didn't I save his life at Cheyenne? That made us quits. And I didn't tell the Marshal because, well, shucks, I had no witnesses and it don't sound a very likely story, does it?'

'No,' say I. 'It don't.'

'Not unless you happened to know Mr Johnston and the strange kind of feller he was. Besides, there's folks in Helena still laying for me over the Plumer business. If I'd gone and confessed, it would have only given them an excuse for stringing me up.'

'The Plumer business,' say I. 'Yeah, that's another instance. I'd dearly like to know the truth about that.'

'You know the truth,' says he, sullen.

'Maybe. But answer me this: Even if you had reasons for not telling the Marshal about Mr Johnston, why couldn't you tell *me*? Why did you give me all that flapdoodle about him leaving town?'

He shrugged. 'I figured it might be best to handle it that way.'

'You figured it might be best!'

'I guess I would have told you later, Missouri. You didn't give me much chance to work round to it.' He threw me a sharp glance. 'How come you know all this, anyway?'

'Haven't I told you: I met Mr Johnston in Helena.'

'Don't give me that stuff!' he yells. 'You flaming liar!'

'How about you, Seth?' says I. 'You know what? I can't be sure of a single word that comes out of your mouth any more.'

'OK,' says he. 'Well, what are you going to do about it? You going to gun me down in cold blood, partner? Or do you plan to give me a fair show?'

'Neither,' says I. 'Not this time. This time I'm going to give you the benefit. Pack your traps and blow. And if I see you any more around Helena . . .'

'Yeah? What'll you do, Missouri, old sport? Call me?' He gave me his most insolent grin. 'It might not be good judgement to call me, being as I'm faster than you are.'

'I can shade you, Seth,' says I. 'Always could, even if you never would admit the fact. Now get your gear and go!'

Seth went away into the shack to gather his belongings and I stood waiting there in the sunlight, my Colt in my hand, ready to see him off the premises for the last time. As I stood there, I began to ponder on how everything had fallen to pieces since I came back from Texas, what with Mr Johnston dead, and Belle turned away from me to marry Quarles, and she never having been what I'd thought her, and Seth a liar and a cheat, and maybe things a whole lot worse than that. I felt so low I was near to weeping, it had all turned out so bad. My gun had drooped a little, I guess, as my attention strayed, but it don't pay to get blue and absent-minded with a Colt in your hand, as the following will make clear:

There I was, feeling sad and lonesome, when suddenly there came a bang and I felt a jolt on my hand. The gun was knocked clean out of it and spun away on to the ground. As for me, the minute I heard that bang I woke from my daydream and went into action. I hunched over and flung myself to one side, reeling considerable so as not to present a steady target. As I did so, I glanced back under my raised arm and got a glimpse of Seth standing in the doorway of the shack with smoke still rising from the muzzle of his gun. He was smiling and looked pleased with himself, the dog. He started to raise his gun again and I reckoned I knew what he had in mind. 'So long, saphead,' he calls out softly.

I lunged for my weapon, got it in my hand and, all in the same movement, I dived for the cover of a big boulder that lay thereabouts, near the bank of the stream. I managed to roll behind that boulder just as Seth loosed off a couple more rounds at me, and I don't think he knew whether he'd hit me or not. He hadn't, but I lay mighty still, hoping he'd come up and investigate. I was able to get a look at him through a fissure in the rock and I could see he was in two minds about what to do. He cocked his head to one side and listened for any sign of life from me.

My gun felt uncommon heavy and my grip was so clumsy I could hardly hold on to it. When I looked down, I saw the reason why: the back of my hand had been ripped open by that slug of Seth's and blood was welling out over everything and trickling down inside my sleeve. I had to take the gun in both hands to steady it, but despite the wound I felt cool and capable now. My head was clear and the danger had raised my spirits. Gunplay is a sure remedy for the miseries, always providing you stay alive long enough to get the benefit.

I think Seth must have heard my movement when I steadied my gun because he started to back away in the direction of his horse, but just when I reckoned I might rise up and return his fire, he loosed off another round to make sure, and the slug struck the top of the rock above my head, and went whining away over the river. Dust drifted down on to my face and one biggish chip flew into my eye, which was plain bad luck. The eye watered, and by the time I'd blinked my way clear of that chip, Seth was on his horse and about to go.

'Here I am, Seth,' yells I. 'Why are you leaving? Come back and face me, you yellow dog!'

Seth fired again to make me keep my head down, and then he set spurs to his horse and went careering away.

'I'll see you again,' I yells after him. 'Make no mistake!' and I stood up and sent a slug of lead in his general direction to show what I had in mind. But he was well away, and as I watched, he took off his hat and waved it in answer. All Seth did, he did in a jolly, insolent way, even when it come to attempts at murder, or running scared.

After he'd disappeared, scouring down the trail, I sat on a rock and nursed my busted hand. I felt I ought to have some deep thinking to do, but not a thought would come into my head. I just sat on there till the sun went down and the cold forced me inside.

9

. . . he returned to his aimless drifting life.

Parting and Meeting

As I say, I went out to one side to think over what had
happened since I came back from Texas, but the only
conclusion I got to was, I didn't mean to stay in Helena no
longer. Like it says in the Book, I meant to shake the dust of
that town off my feet, but first I checked round the place to
make sure Seth had shaken the dust off *his* feet. I figured he
would have, and I was right. There weren't hide nor hair of
that boy, he was clean gone. He never even so much as said
goodbye to Lily, who had been a good friend to him, in her
way. It was Lily came and asked me about Seth, wanting to
know where he'd gone. 'I've got something particular I
want to speak to him about,' says she. I told her I had, too.
But it looked like when Seth lit out from the claim he had
just kept running, and by now he could be anywhere from
Kansas to the Coast. 'Ah well,' says Lily, 'I don't suppose it
matters,' and tackled her drink, and went round the Eagle,
ribbing the customers and fooling about, and did her dance
on stage, like the old days.

But the truth was, it weren't like the old days in the Eagle.
Not to me, anyway. Maybe I just felt that way because Belle
weren't around no more. She and Quarles had gone to
Chicago to find a suitable property where they could live
among his interests. But there was more to it than that. For

instance, Lily felt different. She was still pert and sassy, but there was a desperate air to it all now. Her tongue was sharper than when I first remembered her, and her face was more haggard; there was blue bruises under her eyes, and her cheeks was hollow. Lily didn't look in very good shape, but if you tried to suggest she took it easy, she wouldn't listen, but carried on in the same old reckless style. She would still wear her gunfighter's costume, too, and perform her act, and it's my judgement that if Lily had been a man, she might have turned out to be a formidable gunslinger, being quick and nervous by disposition, and not caring whether she lived or died. She'd either have won a considerable reputation, or else she'd soon have been six feet under.

She and Arthur was the only two left at the Eagle that I remembered from the old times. I stood around in the bar a couple of days and it was full of ghosts. There was Mr Quarles on his little legs, talking sweet and reasonable; and Greg Carter with them green cat's eyes of his, spoiling for a fight; and Handsome Henry Plumer, strutting round in his tooled boots and his broidered vest; and Seth, smiling his smile and leaning up lazy against the bar; and Belle, tall and queenly, waving her hand to call me over. I knew that I had to get out. There weren't nothing left to hold me in Helena, and my mover's blood was stirring.

I figured I wouldn't be coming back that way, so before I left I made Arthur a present of the cabin. It would be somewhere for the boy to live, somewhere to go when he got slung out of the Eagle for looking at the kitchen women with them black breed's eyes of his. Once I'd done that, I rode out. I had money, because Quarles had left me the payment for my quarter share of the cattle, so I just roamed around for a long while, spending it. I suppose you could say that was an 'aimless wandering life' but what's wrong with it? Nothing that I can see. In my experience, most folks don't have too many aims, and maybe they're better off that way. What most folks do is just try to get along; their aims don't reach no higher than a flea's kneecap. All they want to do is keep out of trouble, fill their bellies regular, and maybe have a good supply of whisky. There's only a few folks have aims above that.

Now, Mr Quarles, he had aims. He spent his life plotting and planning for money, but I don't know that he was any the better for it, even if folks such as newspaper editors like to make out he was, and praise him for being 'an astute and upright man of business' and all such stuff. The thing is, if Mr Quarles had been interested in keeping his belly full, there'd have come a time when he'd have had to stop, no matter how much grub was left on the table. He couldn't go on gorging for ever. There was a natural limit. But when it comes to higher aims like making money, Quarles could cram himself for ever, with no limit set. He could sit down and gorge for a lifetime at that table, and he done it, and got praised to the skies for his good works by folks like newspaper editors. If it had been grub he was gorging, he'd have been swole out till he could hardly move, and folks would have said, 'Lord, what a disgusting sight! Look at the shocking old glutton!' But a bank has a bottomless gut. It don't matter how much you shove down there; you can feed it forever. Mr Quarles spent his time doing just that, and he weren't too particular about where the grub came from, either. For instance, I've heard him go on about the Homestead Act a score of times, how he could make it work to his advantage. He used to say what he was doing was no more than good business, but if you want the truth he was hiving that land by his crooked dodges, and robbing ordinary men out of farms, or that's my opinion. It seems strange when you come to think of how folks praised him for doing that, and run round after him, and courted his opinion. What the hell did he want with all that land, anyway?

As to my life being violent after I left Helena, that just ain't so. For a long time I lived the most peaceful life out. I went drifting round from place to place and never had a difference with nobody. When a feller's feeling melancholy and the blues are weighing hard on him, it helps for him to keep on the move, and I reckon that's why I did it. By and by, my cash run out, and then I just took the first job that come to hand. I remembered the tricks I'd learnt on the drive from Texas and I signed on with the Barton Cattle Company. It was a mighty big outfit, the sort where you never see the real boss, and the money has roots that stretch all the way to Chicago or some such place.

I disremember how long I worked for the Barton Cattle Company. Looking back, it seems like a dream, an endless dream full of dust and sweat, and commotion, and fires, and dung, and woodsmoke, and huge starry nights. Maybe you could call that a violent life, in its way, but it was only the violence of the round-up, the violence of the irons in the branding-fires, the rumpus at the cutting out of beasts and the work of the gelding knives. All that dust and dung and blood, and the bellowing of the critturs beating in your ears, that was a sort of violence. Or else there was the violence of the drives to the rail-head, with night stampedes and beasts sucked down in quicksand on the Platte River crossing. It was a tough life, but it weren't violent in no other way.

When I tired of cowpunching, I took on as a bull-waggoner, hauling freight through the mountains, and it was that job took me back. It's strange how you go away from a place and you think you'll never set eyes on it again, nor on the folks there that have hurt you or done you down, but life ain't always so neat, and things don't always work out like that. All this time, I'd been fooling round with the notion of going to the Coast. For a couple of years, it must have been, I told myself I was heading Coastwards, but I never showed the slightest sign of getting there. When I think back, I can see the trouble was that I was always going to set off for the Coast at some other time, in a fortnight or a month, but never then, never that same day. If it was winter, well, I might as well wait for spring; when spring come round, I'd go for certain in the fall. The result was, I never did get to the Coast, and maybe you can draw a lesson from that.

If I'd have gone to the Coast, the rest of what I have to tell would most likely never have come about, though you can't be sure. Anyhow, instead of the Coast, one day I found myself back on the road to Helena with orders to deliver a cargo of freight there. I felt uneasy at first, but there didn't seem any good reason to refuse the trip, and once I was on the way, I found myself growing curious to see the place again.

I rode in there, right down the main street, and it was the strangest thing but I couldn't raise a single face I knew. They was strangers, every one. The town had changed, too. Lots of new buildings had gone up and the place was looking a heap more civilized. It was all pretty depressing. One familiar thing that I did see was a name, 'G. Quarles,' and I seemed to come across that name everywhere. It weren't only on saloons and livery-stables and stores, I even found it on a brass plate outside of a new bank in the square. Mr Quarles might have left Helena but he'd sure left his brand on the place. It looked like he'd gobbled up half the town.

I got rid of my load and went wandering the streets in my free time, asking myself, How can a man come back to a town and not find so much as one familiar face? Then I did find one. I found Arthur's, even if, at first, I hardly recognized it. The face was clean, the black hair slicked down, and he weren't wearing rags any more. He was in a decent coat and pants. In fact, he looked like a clerk.

'Hi, Arthur,' says I. 'You've grown up some since I saw you last.'

He stood and looked at me, frowning, and then he tumbled to who it was. 'Missouri!' he says, and clasped me by the shoulders. 'Am I glad to see you!'

'Same here,' says I, and we just stood grinning at each other for a minute. Then I says, 'This calls for a celebration, Arthur. How does the idea of a drink sound to you?'

'It sounds great,' says he. 'Come on, Missouri. I know a place.'

I followed him down an alley and he led me to an awful ratty-looking shebang.

'Hey,' says I. 'Why'd you pick on a doggery like this?'

'Well,' says Arthur, looking a little uncomfortable. 'They're reasonable, you see. They don't make any trouble. You know how it is.'

Till that moment I'd clean forgot the boy was a breed and might have difficulty getting served in some of the bars, or at best have to stand a lot of jeering talk from them citizens who considered themselves too classy to drink in the same company as breeds.

'OK,' says I, and we went into this two-bit joint and settled down to drink.

'You're looking mighty prosperous, Arthur,' says I.

'You think so?'

'I sure do. I bet you left the Eagle.'

'I got kicked out, Missouri. A long while back.'

It struck me Quarles had done Arthur his best good turn when he stopped being charitable and gave him the boot.

'What you doing now?' says I.

'I work in Berry's, the clothiers. He's a good man. Treats me right well.'

I understood now why Arthur looked so uncommon smart. Old Berry couldn't have him wandering around a gent's outfitters in his rags. It would have been bad for trade.

'I hope you made use of the cabin,' says I.

'I sure did,' says he. 'In fact, I still do.'

'Good. You never heard no more about Seth Walsh, I don't suppose?'

He shook his head. 'And it sounds like you never found him, either.'

'Nope,' says I. 'Not since he gave me this,' and I lifted up my hand with the wide silvery scar along the back of it.

A concerned sort of look came over Arthur's face. 'Listen, Missouri,' says he. 'Could you do me a favour?'

'Spill it,' says I.

'Could you come out with me to the cabin?'

'The thing is, I ain't staying long, Arthur. I'm only passing through.' The truth was that I didn't want to set eyes on that cabin no more. There were too many memories tangled up with it.

'I'd sure appreciate it, if you could spare the time,' says

Arthur. 'There's somebody there I know would like to see you.'

Good Lord, thinks I. Has the boy gone and got himself a wife already? It was all I could think of.

'The sight of an old friend like you would cheer her up.'

'Friend?' says I. 'Who do you mean?'

'Lily.'

'What?' I could hardly believe my ears. 'You mean, Lily's sharing the shack with you?'

'I took her in, Missouri.'

'Took her in? Ain't she at the Eagle?'

He shook his head. 'She's sick,' says he. 'She's had a power of trouble. Come and see her.'

'Well, sure I will,' says I. 'Let's push along there right now.'

We took the trail that led to the cabin and it was an uneasy ride for me, and I don't mean because of my hired mount, though he was made on the ornery side. I still knew the way, of course, but like most everything else round Helena, the trail had changed. It was different in lots of little ways, like, brush had grown up here or been cut back there, a couple of big boulders had been hauled away, a tree had been felled. The trail seemed to be telling me that I was a stranger now, which was unsettling to me. I guess it always is unsettling to go back to a place where you once lived, but what made it worse in my case was, I kept remembering the dark pool up ahead where Mr Johnston had been sunk. I got to picturing that muzzle-bearded face of his, lying in the mud, and them pale eyes glaring up through the water. Sick fancies, but they came clustering round me. I wondered whether Mr Johnston lay there longing for revenge, or whether he was happy with his Blood Atonement; and was it true that he forced Seth's hand? I knew I'd never have the answer to such questions, not for sure. But one thing was certain: Seth had tried to drill me. The scar on my hand was proof enough of that; and what's more, it was always there, to make sure I wouldn't forget.

I followed Arthur in through the cabin door, and he says, 'Got a visitor for you, Lil.'

It was dark in there, out of the sun. I blinked and peered round the dim room, but at first I couldn't see nobody. Then a voice came from the bed under the far window. 'My Lord!' says the voice, all weak and wobbly. 'Don't tell me that's Missouri Fynn!'

I hadn't thought to look in the direction of the bed, but now I did, and what I saw there gave me a monstrous shock. It was Lily, but she was just skin and bone, she'd gone away to nothing. Her cheeks were all hollows and her neck a bundle of cords. Only her eyes had grown bigger. Them brown eyes of hers was so huge now that they seemed to take up half her face. Her hair was still the same, too. It fell in a stream of curls and ringlets, that spread out black across the coverlet, but it looked dry and brittle, and when you got closer you could see the strands of grey running through it. Her hands on the coverlet was lean as paper, and oh! her bony little shoulders. Lily appeared to be in a right bad way.

'It's me, as ever was,' says I. 'How are things, Lily?'

'Take a look – and don't bother to ask,' says she. 'I'm trimmed right down to nothing, ain't I?' and tried to laugh, but the laugh ended in a fit of coughing that took her by the scruff and shook her, like a dog might shake a rabbit.

'Sit down,' says Arthur, and pulled a chair up to the bed for me. 'You and Lily have a talk while I make some coffee.'

Lily held out her hand and I took it between mine. 'Big strong feller,' she murmurs. 'You could break me clean in half. Well, Missouri,' she says, 'if the sight of you don't bring back old times! I'm awful glad to see you. I get kinda lonely now I can't get about.' She cocked her head in the pert way I remembered. 'I'm sulled up here like an ugly old possum,' she says.

'I expect you get company coming.' I thought of all the men she'd known. 'Folks from the Eagle.'

'Used to, but no more. They quit. You can't blame them. I've been on this mattress for six months, and folks forget you after a while.' I saw tears standing at the corners of her eyes. It must have been her general weakness brought them there, because Lily never was one to feel sorry for herself – though God knows, she'd cause to, at that minute.

'There'll be new girls at the Eagle now,' she says, and gave a glance to the peg behind the door, where she'd hung up that smart gunslinger's outfit of hers. She'd kept it, but she wouldn't be needing that no more. Lily had done with all such vanities. I remembered how she used to rip and tear in that costume, what a dash she used to cut, and I felt dreadful sad.

'Arthur's been very kind to me,' she says. 'I have a lot to thank him for. And Belle, too.'

'Belle?' I found the name still gave me a jolt.

'Belle writes, you know. She sends me money from Chicago every now and then. She's very good that way.'

It hurt me to hear Lily talk so humble. 'Does Belle know you're like this?' I asks.

'She knows I'm not well. And she knows about Henry.'

I couldn't work out what Lily meant by that. I figured she must be rambling.

Lily flashed me a smile with a ghost of the old mischief in it. 'Wait till I tell her,' she says. 'Wait till I write and say that I've been paid a call by Missouri Fynn. She'll be green with envy.' Lily ventured a laugh and the cough came back.

'Why, she'll have forgot my name by now.'

'Don't you believe it!' says Lily. 'Only the last letter she wrote, she asked me if I ever saw you. And don't go grinning like that, Missouri, because it's the truth.'

'Yeah.'

'Belle used to dote on you. She was forever talking about you. It was "Missouri this" and "Missouri that". You know what she used to say? She used to tell me to keep my distance from you unless I wanted my eyes scratched out. Belle had a real soft spot for you, Missouri.'

'Well,' says I, 'when it come to the point, she turned me down.'

Lily frowned and looked thoughtful. Then she says, 'Ah, but don't blame her too much. It was a terrible temptation, all that money. Anyhow, look at what's become of me. Belle used to beg me to be sensible, but I would never listen. She warned me, but I just laughed. A woman has to look after herself, Missouri, or she ends up nothing. Like me!'

'Don't say that, Lily.'

'It's true, only I found it out too late. That's why Belle's where she is, and I'm where I am. Don't think too badly of her. She's only human. She's flesh and blood.'

'Yeah, but with Quarles!' says I.

'OK. Sure, he's a freak . . .' Lily was getting so excitable that her cough came back again, and bolted with her like a runaway horse. All she could do was to hold on, and all I could do was to wait for it to wear itself out. 'He's a freak, but his money ain't,' says she when she'd recovered.

'Him and his blasted money!'

'What the hell do you think is keeping *me* now, Missouri?'

'Looks like there's no escaping Quarles and his money-bags,' says I. 'No matter which way we turn.'

'Belle made up her mind not to try,' says Lily. 'Don't put her down for that, Missouri. Don't blame her for being right.'

I hadn't no answer to that, and we sat on for a few minutes without talking, her hand still between mine. It felt like a little cold bundle of twigs.

'Here we are,' says Arthur, coming back. He had a tray in one hand with mugs of coffee on it, and on the other arm he was carrying a young boy, about eighteen months old.

'Come and meet Missouri,' says he to the kid, and set him down gently beside me. The little feller gave me a startled look out of his soft brown eyes and then trundled over to the bed and buried his face in the sheets.

'Aw,' says Lily. 'Don't be scared, Henry.' She took her hand out of mine and fondled the boy's black hair. 'He's shy,' she says to me. 'He don't see many folks.'

'He's been in the water again,' says Arthur.

'You young rip!' says Lily wearily. 'Are you all wet?'

'Just his pants this time,' says Arthur. 'I'll take them off him.'

Henry allowed Arthur to lead him to one side and strip his wet pants off.

I looked enquiringly at Lily.

'That's right,' she says. 'He's mine. There's one reason why I left the Eagle.'

'He looks a fine boy, Lily.'

'He's the sweetest little feller – but he's drawn the marrow out of my bones.'

'Takes after his ma, I can see that. He's got your eyes and your hair, Lily.'

'Yes,' she says. 'I think he does favour me.'

'I hear you called him Henry.'

'That's right.'

'None of my business but – is he Henry Plumer's kid?'

Lily stared down at her hands on the coverlet. She didn't speak for quite a while. Then she says, 'I called him after the man I liked best. God knows, I'd have walked on thorns for Henry. I judge him to have been the most bold, mettlesome feller I've ever struck. Oh, you don't know, Missouri. You can't guess. You only saw one side of Henry Plumer. I idolized that man, even if he did turn out a cheat and a rogue. Anyhow, what's that to me? What do I care if he was an outlaw?' She took a deep breath. 'All the same, the child's not Henry's. If you work out the times, you'll see that Henry Plumer was dead before the baby got started.' She gave me a pale mischievous smile. 'You want to know who his pa was?'

I shrugged.

'Well, you *do* know him, Missouri. You're right well acquainted with him.'

I looked down at the silvery scar on my hand.

'Ain't you going to hazard a guess?'

'I reckon,' says I, 'that it's Seth you're hinting at.'

'You've got it! That's the gentleman!'

Somehow, it hurt me to hear that. 'Didn't you ever tell him?' I asks.

'No,' says Lily. 'I was saving up the good news. Then one day, Seth was clean gone. Just like that. Anyhow, I don't figure he'd have done much about it.'

'Must have happened while I was down in Texas,' says I. All the changes in the world seemed to have come about then.

'Yes,' says Lily. 'That would be right. I used to see a lot of Seth at that time, with him working at the Eagle.'

'What's that?' says I. 'Did he work at the Eagle?'

'Filled in for you, while you was away. I thought you knew about that arrangement.'

'No, Lily. I weren't told.'

'Well, that was the time,' she says, 'and look what come of it,' and slung a loving glance over towards Henry, who was now running round bare-ass, playing some kind of game with Arthur.

'He's the apple of my eye,' says Lily, 'but I get dreadful worried about him.' She was coughing again.

'Why, Lily?'

'Just take a look at me, Missouri. I ask myself, what's going to become of Henry, after . . .'

'Hell! Lily,' says I. 'You'll soon be up and around again.'

She started to tremble and tears fell down her wasted cheeks. 'I'm a bed full of bones,' she says. 'That's what I am. Don't try to fool me with your talk, Missouri – whatever's going to become of the poor mite, after I'm gone?'

'You ain't going nowhere, Lily.'

'That's true,' she says, and her voice was grim. 'I know I'm in this bed to die.' She searched for my hand again, and took hold of it, like the waters was closing over her and she was hanging on to what she could. 'I'm scared,' she whispered. 'Stay with me, Missouri. Help me through it. I'm awful scared.'

I had my job hauling freight, but when she said that, I knew I wouldn't be going back to it for a while. A man has to be awful busy to turn down a request like the one Lily made to me.

'I'll stick around,' says I. 'You can count on that.'

She laid her head back on the pillow and her eyelids drooped. 'You know,' she murmurs, 'Belle was right. You *are* a sweet-natured feller,' and in another minute she was asleep.

10

. . . an orphan child. . . .

My Promise About Young Henry

I stayed at the cabin for weeks. I couldn't think of going till
Lily had made it one way or another, and it soon became
clear that I was there to help her into the grave. Every day
she got weaker, and what flesh of hers was left, melted away.
Her eyes grew big and staring, and sometimes when she
coughed she would retch bright blood. Lift her up to clean
her and you'd find the poor soul didn't hardly weigh
heavier than a bird. She'd dwindled down to nothing, the
merest wisp, a feather and a bone.

Sometimes, in the later days, she rambled, and then she
talked to Henry Plumer most, and it was like he sometimes
talked back to her. It was creepy, I can tell you, to hear her
exchanging endearments with a man already gone to dust.
Who would have guessed there was such deep feeling
between them? Not me, at the time. I guess I was wrapped
up in my own affairs, and just didn't allow that there could
be so much of passion where there was so little that was
solemn. How the poor girl must have suffered when they
took Henry Plumer to the hanging-tree. Two things I learnt
from listening to Lily: First, not to judge by outward
appearances in matters of love, and second, not ever to
imagine that a man needs to be decent or upright to win the
heart of a woman. It just ain't so.

Now and then, Lily would come back to her senses, and then she would talk in her pert old style. One day, she told me about how she left the Eagle, and was taken in by a feller called Ben Parker. 'You won't know him,' she says, 'and you can count that as your good luck. Well, he comes along and tells me I'm the girl of his dreams. I was carrying young Henry at that time, so I gave him that information in exchange, but he says it don't matter. I didn't know where to turn just then, and I was awful lonesome, so I went with him. My God, what a slob Ben Parker turned out to be! Honest, you have *no* idea. He was the most insulting man breathing. Do you know, he'd come back home with a skinful of whisky, drag me off to bed, and then fall asleep on *top* of me! I've had to wrestle my way out from under the drunken bum more times than I care to remember. Ain't men just pigs!'

'Not all of us are like that, Lily.'

'No,' says she. 'Some of you manage to keep awake. But I'll let you in on a secret, Missouri: I never cared too much for all that business that goes on behind the bedroom door.'

I couldn't help but smile, remembering Lily when she was young and skittish, sitting on Henry Plumer's knee, laughing like mad, her face all flushed with excitement and liquor. Maybe she hadn't thought too much of it since Henry went, but at that time she did, or else I'm a Dutchman!

'What happened to Parker?' says I.

'He ditched me,' says Lily. 'What do you think? After a few months, when I was all swole up, he comes in and says he's leaving. "You're no use to me," he says. No use! after what I'd had to put up with from that pig of a man. "Anyhow," he says, "I've found the girl of my dreams." "What, again?" says I. "Who is it this time?" "Her name's

Phyllis, if you must know," says he. "She's working at the Tin Whistle just at present, but I mean to take her away from all that, and give her a new life." I suppose that means he's falling asleep on top of Phyllis now, poor girl.' Lily heaved a sigh. 'Oh, Missouri,' she says, 'to have to wear your life out with such rubbish!'

I used to sit looking at Lily sometimes when she lay back on her pillow, drowned in sleep, and I used to think how strange it was that I should be the one to sit by her now. Of all the men she'd known, of all the fellers that had chased her or pined for her, the ones she'd let into her bed and them she'd turned away, there was nobody left. There was only me, who had been a friend, but had never gone with Lily, and never would now, because she was fading away before my eyes.

As time passed, little Henry lost his shyness with me and we got along just fine. I was around the place a lot more than Arthur, who had to go to his work every day, so naturally I ran the house and looked after the kid. He was a cheery, good-natured soul most times, but now and then he'd get up to some monkey-business, and when I saw such sly devilment in so young a shaver, I couldn't help but think: There's his pa's blood coming out in him. Strangely enough, I liked him all the better for it.

Lily used to fret a good deal about young Henry, and wake in the night to weep for his future. It used to worry me, too, for it weren't clear what would happen to him. One day, when she was tearing herself to pieces about the boy, a thought struck me. 'Listen,' says I. 'Why don't you ask Belle to care for Henry? – in case anything should happen to you, I mean.'

Lily gave me a scornful look for adding that last remark,

but I didn't like to talk about her death in front of her. It didn't seem decent, though I knew she was a goner. I'd called a doctor in for his opinion, and he says to me in private: 'There's not a thing I can do for her. I'm sorry. She's in the last stages of consumption. You've got to face the fact that she's dying.' Well, I knew that already, but you always hope a medical man will come up with something, though it don't often happen.

'Belle?' says Lily. 'Yes. Yes. Yes. I could ask Belle.' She was feverish, near to raving. 'Belle's got the wherewithal. Do you reckon she . . . ? She could give him a real good home, couldn't she? Yes. A real good home.' She sat bolt upright, her feeble frame a-tremble and her huge eyes staring. 'I got to write to her,' she says.

'Sure. Take it easy.'

'I'd better write to her now.'

Lily asked me to look in the top drawer of the chest-of-drawers next to her bed, to get Belle's letters out from there so that she could see the address. It took me a little while to locate them letters, and by the time I had, Lily had fallen back on the pillow and was out cold. It was more like she'd been slugged than gone to sleep. I took a peek at the top page of the letters and saw that Belle had been writing all about her life in Chicago, how she and George owned this big brownstone house, and how they went to dinner-parties with all the best people, and how life was just one long social whirl, and such fun! I didn't read no more. It seemed wrong to be reading of such things with Lily on her death-bed. I felt my cheeks burn, like I'd been caught spying on secrets, and there was a dull pain in my chest. I put the letters back in the drawer till they should be needed.

Lily never got round to writing that letter. Next day she

died. She knew she was going, and fought to speak when she was on the edge of eternity. It was Henry that was in her mind. She made me promise to write to Belle about young Henry, and when that was over, she lay back and gave a twisted little smile and says, 'You know what, Missouri? I don't think I got a fair shake in my life,' and with that, she died. She just slipped away, there weren't no more fighting. Her fingers went limp as they lay in mine, and she was gone. I was glad she went so easy. She stepped out of life like she might kick off a pair of shoes, once her mind was at rest about Henry.

Two days later we followed her to the graveyard. There was me, and Arthur, and little Henry hanging on to our hands, not understanding what was happening. That was all the mourners we could muster. We left her under a cross carved with her death-date and the words 'Lily Farmer, mother of Henry.' That's it, thinks I, as we walked away. That's the end of little Lily. She couldn't have been more than twenty-five. It made no sense at all.

Back at the cabin, I put the orphaned child to bed, got out Belle's letters and wrote explaining matters to her, as I'd promised I would. That's how fate takes a hand, and drives us on to places we'd never have got to of our own accord. The address in Chicago was 'Riverside Drive'.

It might be thought that fate would have allowed Mr and Mrs Quarles to live in peace after their removal to Chicago.

Taking Henry to Chicago

Me and Henry lived with Arthur while we was waiting for an answer from Chicago. The reply was so long coming that I'd come to the conclusion my letter had never reached Belle and was just working myself up for another try when a letter from her did arrive, on pink paper and smelling of roses. Belle wrote how glad she was to hear from me and how depressing she found the news of Lily's death, and says I was to bring young Henry to join her and Mr Quarles in Chicago as soon as possible. Let her know the time of arrival and she'd meet us at the station, says she. It was a handsome offer. She even sent along the fares, which was good judgement, because by that time I was all on broke.

We went on that eastbound train, Henry and me, and it took us away from the mountains on to the great flat plains of Nebraska and Iowa on our way to Illinois. When at last we ran into Chicago, I felt a strange clenching in my chest at the sight of that huge city unrolling on either side of the line. There was so much of it, such mazes of streets, so many tall chimneys, so much smoke and stone and brick and iron, it felt like we was running into a monstrous cage.

We stood there on the platform, and I don't know about

young Henry, but I was sure feeling lost. The locomotive was hissing, and every now and then it pushed out shrieking jets of steam, trolleys was rumbling around and crowds of folks with pale faces was rushing everywhere. I never seen so many suits in all my life – the men looked like a field of crows. I begun to feel awful conspicuous, standing there in my tall boots and canvas jacket and my beat-up hat, but I needn't have worried. Folks just looked right through me, and their faces wore the usual expression, which was a blank.

We'd have been standing there yet, I guess, if Belle hadn't turned up. I spotted her when she was still some way down the platform. In fact, you couldn't miss her. It weren't just that she *looked* different from the run of folks, she even *moved* in a different style. They was all scurrying around, but she came gliding up like she'd all the time in the world, and the others, they made way for her, they gave her the road. She was all shining satins and flounces of lace, and on her head, riding above her golden hair, a hat with blue ostrich plumes that made her look about ten feet tall.

'There you are, Missouri,' says she, coming sweeping up on us. 'How *lovely* to see you again. Aren't you going to give me a kiss?'

She leant forward and I planted a kiss on her cheek. It was smooth and pale, dusted over with powder. She smelt like a flower. Scent hung round her in a cloud, like she had her own sweet personal world, separate from the rest of us bums.

'My! You're prickly as a porcupine,' says she.

'Sorry, Belle. I ain't had a chance for a shave lately.'

'Don't apologize. I like it,' says she with a grin. 'Now, let's have a look at you.' She walked right round me, surveying me, which put me out a little, somehow.

'I was *so* sorry to hear about Lily,' says she, coming to

rest. 'Wasn't it tragic? – but I must say, you're looking well, Missouri. It gives me quite a thrill to see you again, standing there in your high boots and your canvas jacket. How *are* you?'

It struck me Belle had got to be a more fancy talker.

'Fine,' says I. 'Here's the boy,' and I pushed him forward.

'Oh,' says Belle. 'What a cute little feller! Aren't you a cute little feller? He has a look of his ma. Yes he does, I can see it plain! Are you going to come and stay with your auntie Belle? – What's his name again, Missouri?'

'Henry.'

'You going to come and stay with your aunt Belle, Henry?'

Henry held his tongue and looked like he might be reserving his judgement.

Belle fluttered a hand, and I noticed she was wearing cotton gloves of the palest lavender. In answer to her signal, out stepped a tall young man from behind her and handed her a big box tied up with ribbon. 'Thanks, Richard,' says she.

This Richard was a mighty nifty dresser. He was wearing a tall hat and grey tail-coat and a frilly white shirt on which unfortunately a few smuts had lodged from the soot in the air. I guessed Richard must be a member of the family, or else a friend.

'Here you are, young Henry,' says Belle, handing him the box. 'I expect you like candy.'

Henry took hold of that box, which was durn near as big as him, and he grinned over the top of it at Belle, and that's the way the ice first got broken between them.

'All right, Richard,' says Belle. 'You can drive us home now.'

It weren't till I saw him up on the box that I realized Richard was the coachman. Still, Belle was mighty nice and considerate to him, and treated him almost like he was a friend.

'Take us round the long way,' says Belle. 'Let's show our visitors a little of what we've got here, Richard.'

What they'd got was shops, strung out along a street that seemed to go on for ever, shops jammed with all the treasures of the world. There was some huge buildings, too: churches and halls and offices. And there was miles and miles of cobbled road.

'Chicago!' says Belle. 'Don't you just love it? The most wide-open city in the entire Union!'

I couldn't say I was struck with it on a first viewing, and when we came to a poorer quarter, I liked it a whole lot less. The light that come down from the rooftops was yellowish. The stone of the factories was black and sweaty. There was a smell of sulphur, and of something else that came creeping along – the stink of burning hooves and hide, like the breath of wickedness itself. Just then, a hooter wailed and out of the factory gates streamed a world of folks, all in greasy clothes, all their faces pale and sickly-looking, and most with the same blank stare that I'd noticed before.

'They don't look as if they love it,' says I.

'They do all right,' says Belle. 'Take my word for it. They earn good money. You'd be surprised. Better than a man could get in Helena or sod-busting on the plains. We'll soon be out of this area, anyway.'

'Yeah,' says I, but I knew that Chicago weren't no place for me.

Before long, we ran into a stretch where it was all wide roads and large houses and green lawns and trees. Belle pointed up ahead and says, 'That's it!' and I saw a place big enough to quarter a regiment, a huge mansion built of stone. 'That's the Quarles residence,' says Belle. 'What do you think of it?'

'A trifle on the large side, ain't it, Belle?'

'Yeah well,' she says. 'It *has* to be, doesn't it?'

I couldn't for the life of me figure out why, when there was only Quarles and her living there, but when I got inside I reckoned they must need it to house the servants. They'd got a great pack of servants running round the place, they were swarming everywhere, and you couldn't so much as walk through the door without servants trying to get the coat off your back or help you into a chair.

'Let's go into the drawing-room,' says Belle, and led me into a place about the size of a church hall. It was full of gilded chairs and sofas with carved wood. There was marble pillars holding up the fancy plaster of the ceiling and a marble fireplace big enough to roast an ox. Over the mantelpiece there was the biggest painting I'd ever set eyes on. It was enormous, and it was a picture of George Quarles. He was looking mighty sombre and dignified, with one hand in his lapel, and the other appearing to rest on the top of what was a model of a building. He was about ten feet tall in the picture.

'George appears to have done some growing since he settled in Chicago,' says I.

'Oh that,' says Belle. 'That's George posing as a City Father.' She went over to the wall and yanked at a length of silky rope that was hanging there, and in walked a nurse in full uniform.

'This is Marietta,' says Belle. 'She's going to take charge of young Henry. Take the boy along now and show him the nursery.'

Marietta gave a curtsey, took young Henry by the hand and led him out of the room. I guess the boy was in a daze by this time: he let himself be carried off by this stranger and never raised a murmur in complaint.

'Who was it got the kid on Lily?' says Belle, as soon as he was out of the room.

'I don't know.'

'Mm,' says she. 'Well, I guess you'll want to remain with us a day or two, while Henry settles in?'

'If that's OK.'

'Of course it is. I expected it. I've had a room made ready. Come on, Missouri. I'll show it you.'

She took me by the hand and led me across the hall, and that had some surprises in it, too, like statues of naked young bucks and handsome ladies with their only garment falling off them.

'Hey,' says I. 'That's fun.'

'No, it ain't,' says Belle. 'It's Art. And it's dead serious.'

I couldn't help but laugh when I thought of all the high-toned folks that must look at them statues, folks like preachers and bankers and society dames. I suppose they'd come in and have a good stare at what was on show, and say, 'Very fine,' and 'A remarkable piece of work,' and never turn a hair at seeing young women with their boobs swinging free, nor bare-assed studs, neither, so long as they was carved in stone. Put real ones in their place and they'd have run mad. Why? I asked Belle and she says because in stone it was Art, and that made all the difference.

She led me up a wide, curving staircase with fancy railings of worked iron. There was a lot of paintings hung on the walls, but these were pictures of ordinary things such as waggon-trains and Injuns and the South Pass in the Rockies.

'Mr Quarles appears to have got very partial to paintings,' says I.

'Yeah,' says she. 'George has taken up Art in a big way.'

'You mean he's *painting* these here?'

Belle bust out laughing. 'Can you see it! No, he's not painting them, Missouri, he's buying them.'

'Is that a fact!'

'He went into it all, and what he came up with was, Art ain't only a good investment but it also adds tone to a place, and that's a combination you just can't beat.'

'You mean to tell me these are worth money, Belle? All these pictures of carts, and waggons, and Injun squaws?'

'Sure they are! Maybe you don't know it,' says she, 'but back here in Chicago there's a great vogue for the West, and all to do with it.'

'And Mr Quarles, he's got this vogue, has he?'

'I'll tell you, Missouri,' says she, 'George has grown mighty fond of the West since he came back East. He brags about living out there.' She gave a laugh. 'What's more, if he catches sight of you in that canvas jacket, he'll most likely want you for his Western Museum. – But don't worry, cowboy, he'll offer you a good price!'

'What are you jawing about, Belle?'

'Come on,' says she. 'I'll show you. His collection's in the gallery.'

She took me into a long, long room, the sides of which was lined with items like old-style Colts, and one-shot carbines, and Spanish spurs, and them Mexican saddles with a big hump of ironwood, and a war-bonnet from some Sioux chief, and bows and arrows with different featherings, and beat-out mining tools, and a satchel stamped with the words, 'Pony Express', and a heap of other things besides, big and little, from waggons to bullet moulds.

'Don't tell me all *this* is Art,' says I, 'or else I've been living plumb in the middle of Art all my days without once suspicioning the fact!'

'George says this ain't Art yet, but give it a little time and it'll turn into Art, and it grows in value every day.'

'Well, you've got me stumped,' says I. Then among the hats and *coup* sticks and pictures hanging on the wall I noticed an old Army tunic, shabby and torn, and under it a card reading: 'Recovered from Iron Dog, war-chief of the Dakota, twelve months after the disaster that befell General Custer on the Little Big Horn.' Looking at that tunic, with its rents and old bloodstains, I was put in mind of certain other items I'd once seen in Mr Quarles's possession.

'I don't see no bloody shirts nor hempen ropes nowadays,' says I.

'He's still got 'em,' says Belle. 'They're in what he calls his "Black Museum". He keeps them out of sight because they tend to upset the Chicago ladies.'

She showed me the little room to one side where Mr Quarles housed his 'Black Museum'. We had to unlock the door before we could get in. It was stacked, inside, with the same sort of bloodstained trophies as I remembered seeing, but there had been plenty of additions, and among them was Henry Plumer's boots. It gave me quite a jolt to see them tooled leather boots, still in prime condition, but I kept quiet and said nothing.

'The West's George's hobby,' says Belle, leading me back up the stairs. 'And Western paintings in particular. You know he gets top-rate artists to work for him. "Commissioning", they call it. He likes to be talked of as a patron of the Arts.'

'He does?'

'They wrote a piece about him in the *Mirror*, not long ago: "Mr G. Quarles, Outstanding Patron of the Arts". Mind you, that ain't too surprising. George owns a big slice of the *Mirror*.'

'And what do you think of it all, Belle?'

'Me?' she says, offhand. 'Oh, I think it's very interesting.'

She showed me to my bedroom which was as big as a fair-sized barn, but not done out like one, not by a long sight. Everything was sweet and clean, and the furniture was glowing mahogany, and the carpets soft. I felt almost shamed to see my ratty old carpet-bag standing by the bed. Richard or another of the servants must have brought it up.

'My! You really do look good!' says Belle, and stood close to me.

'You mean, good for a saddle bum,' says I, joking.

'Well,' says she, pretending to consider, 'any woman that was partial to gaunt, bow-legged, leather-faced young ruffians would go for you. I'll say that much.'

'Thanks,' says I. 'You're right complimentary.'

'Well,' she says, 'at least you look like a man. Smell like one, too.' And she put her scented face down to my shirt, and laid her cheek against my chest. 'Mm,' she says, 'That shirt is full of good smells.'

I gave an uneasy laugh. 'Such as what?'

'Such as sage-brush and whisky and cheap cigars. You know what, Missouri, you smell like a night at the Eagle.'

'The Eagle,' says I. 'I thought you'd have forgot all that.'

She went on sniffing. 'Smells like gunsmoke and saddle leather.'

'You know,' says I, 'it sounds like you've got it worse than Mr Quarles. I'll tell you what this shirt smells of, it smells of sweat, on account of it ain't been off my back in days.'

'All right,' she murmurs. 'But man's sweat. Hard riding sweat.' Her fingers was running softly in my hair.

'Listen here, Belle,' says I, breaking free. 'I'm going to make you a present of this shirt: You think a sight more of it than I do!'

I stood clear of her. I weren't willing that Belle should pick me up like a toy and play with me just because it suited her whim. But all the same, my heart was beating hard at the touch of them remembered fingers.

Belle laughed and let the matter go, and we went back to the drawing-room and was taking tea there – which was a moderately new experience for one of us – when in walked Mr Quarles. He was a busy man and he looked it. He came humming in like a bee on them little legs of his. When he saw me sitting there, he gave a quick glance at his fob watch, as if to say, 'I can spare you five minutes, pal, or maybe even ten, for old times' sake.'

Mr Quarles didn't look very different, save that his back had got a little rounder and his belly was slung a trifle closer to his knees. The only real change in him was that when he talked now he sometimes made a whistling noise. I took a look at his mouth and saw that his teeth was all white and sparkling. Quarles had used to have yellow teeth with a mossy appearance up by the gums, but they was gone and in their place was snow white teeth that had a slight whistle about them. I figured they must be another recent acquisition, and that he was still breaking them in. Apart from the teeth, he was much the same. He didn't look powerful nor important, nor even dignified, like he did in the picture. He was just a little fat man, and looked harmless – which might have been one of his best weapons, when you come to think.

Quarles came and shook my hand, and says something about how good it was to see me again, and that I looked 'a true man of the West'. Rubbish of that kind came easy to him. 'How's it been, Missouri?' says he, not waiting for an answer before moving on to his next question. 'You still wandering around? Can't settle, huh? What do you say you've been doing? If you've been punching cattle, maybe you've worked for one of my outfits, The Barton Cattle Company? Yep, I got an interest. They don't all come wearing my name, you know. Ha ha. You ain't got round to marrying yet? Well, there's time, there's time. But I know you young miners and hard riders, you just got to bust out every now and then. Saddle fever, huh? I admire it, and it's been the making of the West, but it don't help a man to settle. I've always said, and I'll say it again now, Missouri, you've got a bright future ahead of you, if you can only settle down and work for it.' He gave a sigh. 'Still getting by in the same old style.' He shook his head and his dewlaps wobbled.

'I guess we're all doing that, Mr Quarles.'

'– Call me George. I think you've got to allow that *we've* changed. Look at all this,' and he waved his hand round the room in a proud way.

'I reckon you're still hunting after the next dollar, Mr Quarles. That's still the same.'

'It's not the money now, Missouri,' says he, and a kind of religious light shone in them prune-dark eyes of his. 'Come over to the window, boy. Take a look out there. That's what it's about for me now. Just look at that city!'

'Yeah.'

'You see, Missouri, I'm helping to make all that. My capital is helping to *create* that city. I'm one of the few men privileged to play such a role, and I can tell you, the responsibility is a great one.'

'I guess you're right, Mr Quarles. You have changed.'

'And you could change, too,' says Quarles. He was going at me like a preacher. 'Others that were cast in the same mould as you, they've changed. You know that? There's a place for a young man with your talents in Chicago . . .'

'Such as what?' says I.

'Well, we have to safeguard our interests here, same as anywhere else. There'd be openings, believe me. You know, you ought to think over your future, Missouri, and if . . .'

'– Don't you want to see the little boy?' says Belle, breaking in. 'Shall I ring for him?'

Quarles looked at his watch. 'Not now, dear,' says he, 'I haven't got the time.'

'It's right friendly of you,' says I, 'taking Henry in like this. I want to thank you.'

'Think nothing of it. It'll give Belle something to occupy her. Well, I must go.' He set off and then stopped and came back and shook hands. 'By the way,' says he, looking me up and down, 'tomorrow night I happen to be holding a reception; I'll be showing off my latest buy in the Art field, and I can guarantee it's going to be a big social occasion. I don't know whether you'd . . . ?'

'Heck!' says Belle. 'Don't bother him with such questions now. The poor man's only just arrived off the train. Let him get his bearings, George.'

'Yeah. You're right. Well, I have to go. Make yourself at home, Missouri. So long,' and he went humming away.

'Mr Quarles keeps pretty lively,' says I.

'Oh yes,' says Belle. 'He's brisk as a body louse, is George.'

'Weren't that strange?' says I. 'He almost sounded like he was offering me a job, straight off.'

Belle leant back lazy on the sofa. 'You know, Missouri,' she drawls, 'you look simply *dee*-licious with that long hair a-swishing round your collar. The kind of sharks we get round here, they all wear it so short and mean.'

What kind of an answer was that? I left Belle and went up to my room and unpacked my shirts – both of them. Well, thinks I, maybe Chicago ain't the place for you, Missouri, but it sure looks like young Henry's going to get a good start in life. 'Pleased with that, Lily?' says I to the ceiling. I was damn sure she would be.

12

If we ask ourselves whose was the responsibility for the bloody affray at Riverside Drive, there is only one answer possible ... the trouble was deliberately provoked by Fynn and the subsequent murder and wounding were of his doing. It was a barbarous act, a blow against all civilized standards, carried out as it was among a gathering including some of Chicago's most eminent citizens.

A True Show, all Fair and Square

'I guess you won't be wanting to attend the reception?' says Belle to me the next day.

'Dead right!' says I. 'That kind of thing ain't my style. On the other hand, I wouldn't want to offend Mr Quarles, not when he's been so kind and all.' I'd just seen young Henry being taken off for a walk by Marietta, the nurse, and the boy looked right happy and cheerful. I didn't want to threaten that arrangement in any way.

'Oh, don't worry about George,' says Belle. 'You know what it'll be tonight, Missouri? It'll be the dinner-parties all over again: fancy clothes and polite conversation.' She gave me a wink. 'I take it you won't be putting in an appearance?'

'Not by choice, Belle.'

'I'll tell you your best plan. Say nothing to nobody but just slip away. Then you can't be roped in.'

'Makes sense, Belle.'

'Sure it does. Go down into Chicago for the evening, why don't you? Take a look at the big city. See the sights.'

'Yeah,' says I, 'that's what I think I will do,' and I did, and took with me most of what little money I had left, which turned out to be a big mistake.

I was in the main streets of the city to begin with, where the lighting was a marvel, bright as day, and the shops still bustling with customers. I wandered round for a while and then I thought I'd like a drink so I looked round for a bar. I found one and went inside, and it was all red plush and brass rails, and smart fellers sitting round at tables with marble tops and talking low. I ranged up to the bar and asked for a whisky but the feller doing the serving didn't seem to notice me. I stood there for a while, watching other men get attended to, and then I says, 'Pardon me, but I called for a whisky. Why don't you serve me?'

The bartender looked right through me. I might as well not have been there.

'Hey, I'm talking to you!' says I.

'Excuse me,' says the bartender in a tight little voice, 'but I'm occupied at the moment.'

'Well, I'm next,' says I. 'Don't you forget that now,' and gave him a smile. I weren't looking for any difficulty.

He finished the order he was making up and then he slipped away through a door at the rear of the bar. A minute after, in comes the softest, podgiest, sleekest gentleman, with rings on his fingers and a flower in his buttonhole. He glided up to me and leant his head near mine, right confidential. 'I'm sorry, sir,' says he in a pleasant murmur, 'but we're unable to serve you.' I could smell cachous on his breath, he was that close.

'Why not?'

'It's your mode of dress, sir. We observe certain rules here. We keep to certain, ah, standards. If you see what I mean.'

'My dress?' I looked at myself in the mirror that covered the back wall of the bar, and I did see what he meant. There was I in my canvas jacket in the middle of an empty space. Everybody else was in dark suits and they had backed right off me, like I had the smallpox.

'Who are *you*?' says I.

'It happens that I'm the proprietor. Now, I'm sure you won't want to cause any trouble. It's simply a rule of the house. Nothing personal, you understand.'

'OK, Mr Proprietor,' says I, 'but I think I should have that one drink first.'

A kind of ape in a dress-suit loomed up behind the proprietor and gave him an enquiring glance.

The proprietor looked me up and down, then he says, 'All right, just the one,' and waved the human ape away, but he didn't go far. He stood about three paces off while I tackled my whisky, and when I left, he lumbered after me. When I reached the door, there was the proprietor, pleasant as you like, bowing me out and saying in his mild, milky voice, 'Profound apologies. I regret that we couldn't accommodate you, sir,' sounding for all the world like an old-style gentleman, and the ape looming over his shoulder.

After that experience I made up my mind to find some place a little less high-toned to do my drinking in. I strayed here and there, and I must have wandered into a poor section because before long it was all tenements and factory gates and blank brick walls. The lighting was more feeble here, and the back-alleys ran away in all directions. The place was swarming with folks, and there was considerable

143

numbers of loafers and drunks around. The air smelt kind of used up, maybe because there was so many people going at it, and the garbage in the gutters was pretty ripe, too. There was kids shinning around everywhere, some of them looking as raggedy as Arthur when I first met him, and there was old folks, too, that weren't in much better shape. Rummies stood at the entrance to saloons, wheedling for dimes, and old ladies in shawls was panhandling on street corners. In one place I saw what looked like a heap of corpses lying on the sidewalk, up against the wall, with folks just passing by and almost stepping on them, but paying them no attention. I went up to see, and they weren't dead, they were asleep, lying on an iron grating with hot air coming up through the bars from the bakehouse below. That was their bed for the night, poor souls. When I saw such things, I got uneasy: it weren't what I'd been led to expect of Chicago.

Here and there was women standing in doorways, their bosoms hanging out, and as you passed they'd call in wheedling voices, 'Come on, honey. Have some fun!' and then sling the worst kind of language after you, if you kept on going. A young girl came up to me, selling matches off a tray, a peaky little creature she was, no more than eleven years old, with dark hair and a face as white as chalk. I let her sell me a box of matches, and then she wanted to sell me something else!

'You shouldn't be roaming round like this,' say I. 'Where are your folks?'

She gave me a look as sharp as a needle. 'What are you? The cops?' she jeers. Then she says, 'I'll do it for a dollar.'

'Do what, honey?'

'You name it, mister,' she says. Oh, there was a desperate swagger about her.

'Here,' says I, and I gave her the dollar and told her to cut along home, but I don't imagine she went.

I was feeling pretty low by this time so I turned into a drinking-shop. Believe me, it was Babel in there, with every kind of different lingo being talked, but at least I could buy myself a whisky without trouble. Folks was more friendly, altogether, and it weren't long before I struck up a conversation with a couple of young fellers, name of Pete and Dick. They was mighty pleasant, and very interested to hear that I'd just come all the way from Montana. I didn't mention Mr and Mrs Quarles and the fact that I was staying at a tony address like Riverside Drive. I figured they'd only think I was bragging and telling monstrous lies.

'Have you been to Charlie's Place?' asks Pete, after a while. 'You got to come along to Charlie's, it's the most bully place out.'

'OK,' says I. 'Let's go there.'

We set off, and I judged Pete and Dick must have been drinking a while before they run into me, the way they started yelling and wrestling and generally horsing around on the way to Charlie's, which was down a narrow alley.

Charlie's Place didn't look much from the outside, but that didn't matter. 'Come on, boys,' says I. 'This round's on me,' and I led the way through the door and up to the bar. I put my hand in my pocket to take out my money, and it had gone. I turned round to explain matters to my pals, and they had gone, too. There weren't a sign of them anywhere. I ran back into the alley and looked up and down but they had vanished. It was a mean trick, and I felt pretty let down by Dick and Pete.

There I was, in the middle of Chicago, without a cent in my pocket. Well, I mooched around a while longer, but what was the use? I didn't even like it there. Nothing else was left but to go back to Quarles's and hope to slip up to my room without being spotted. I weren't feeling in any mood for party-going nor social chit-chat.

I had trouble getting back into Quarles's house, too. There was a strong-man on the door, another ape, but tricked out in gold braid this time. When I tried to argue with him, he was all for pitching me down the stairs, but luckily, at that moment, Mr Quarles came along. 'That's OK, Jarman,' says he. 'Let him through. He's a friend of the family,' and then the ape was all smiles, and bowed, and even gave me a salute. Can you beat it!

'Where've you been, Missouri?' says Quarles. 'I've been looking for you. There's one or two people I'd like to introduce you to.'

'Hadn't I better get some different clothes on first?' I didn't mention that I hadn't got no other clothes. All I wanted was to make it to my room.

'No, stay as you are,' says Quarles. 'They'll be interested to see you in your present outfit.'

We was standing in the doorway of the drawing-room by now. The place was packed with ladies and gentlemen, the men in black suits and the ladies shining and glittering in long dresses, with ropes of pearls about their throats, and bare white shoulders. It struck me how many lovely women there was amongst this crowd, and what a beat-up lot the men was, by the side of them. It was like the ladies had bloomed extra well in Chicago, but the men had dwindled down and got near-sighted and podgy.

'Take a look round,' says Quarles, with his proud voice on again. 'This is a very distinguished gathering we've got here.'

'I'll bet,' says I.

'Cast your eyes round this room, Missouri, and you'll find most of the men that count in Chicago.'

'Count? How do you mean, count?'

'They run it, Missouri. They carry a heavy burden, believe me. Look,' says he. 'There's Mervyn Gliddon, he's Barbed Wire. And there's Edwin Thomas, he's Armour Packing. And there's Hiram Jobson, MacCormick Reapers. And Jacob Wild, Real Estate.'

'Where's Belle?' says I, thinking that at least I could talk to her.

'Belle? She's assisting with the arrangements in the gallery.' He gave me a smile from his perfect new teeth. 'You're in time for the unveiling, anyway. I think you'll find that interesting.' He laughed and twinkled his eyes at me.

I must have looked blank, because he goes on, 'The new picture. The one that I commissioned from Mr Lascelles, I'm putting it on display. You ever hear of Mr Lascelles?'

'Can't say I did, Mr Quarles.'

'He's – oh, never mind. But you ain't got a drink, Missouri. Where are those blamed waiters? Ah, there's Harold Oxley.' He pointed to a little grey-haired man that was wandering by. 'Harold's big in Grain. Harold, hello!'

Harold turned and nodded.

'Come and meet a friend of mine, Harold,' says Quarles. 'This is Missouri Fynn, a real tough young Westerner. I've known him since the days when I was out there myself. Montana, that was, you'll remember.'

Harold shook hands with me.

'You two have a talk,' says Quarles. 'I'll go and see if I can rustle up some drinks. These durn waiters, they're all cripples!' Then, just as he was going, he turned to Harold and whispers, 'Mind what you say to Missouri. He's a handy man with a gun,' and off he went, laughing.

Harold gave me a startled look, and then he decided it was a joke. 'You in farming?' he asks.

'Farming?' says I. 'No.'

'Cattle business?'

'I have done something in that line.'

'What sort of spread you got?'

'No spread, Mr Oxley. I was a cowhand.'

'Ah,' says he, and stared into his empty glass. Talk kind of died between us after that, and we just stood there. Nothing in common, I guess. I was glad when Mr Quarles came back with the drinks and rescued us from each other.

Mr Quarles's next introductions went better to start with. He took me over to a little group of ladies that I'd seen already casting glances at us. Mr Quarles made his little speech about me, which was another load of flapdoodle: 'I just can't tell you all that Missouri's done,' says he. 'The gold-mining, and cowpunching – and the gunfighting, too.'

The ladies all looked mighty interested at that, and pursed up their red mouths, and asked a lot of fool questions. There was two of them in particular that stuck with me when the others drifted off or was called away by their menfolk. There was Mrs Thomas, who was plump and wide-eyed, and liked to act the innocent, though she must have been well turned thirty, and there was Mrs Race, who was dark-haired and thin, and kind of hungry about the cheekbones. Mrs Race had a low purring voice and a slinky manner, and a way of smiling that called Seth to mind.

The way they asked me about life out West, it was as if they thought of it as some kind of zoo or raree show. I did my best to keep my answers polite, but it weren't easy. Then Mrs Thomas says, 'That shirt . . .'

'I'm sorry about the shirt, ma'am,' says I. 'You see, I weren't reckoning on . . .'

'Oh, don't apologize,' says Mrs Thomas. 'I think it looks simply wonderful. And the jacket! Do men *really* go about like that out West?'

'I suppose they do.'

'And wear those big hats, like in the illustrations?'

'Some of them do, ma'am.'

'And the high boots like you've got on. And the spurs. Do *you* wear spurs?'

'Not to parties, ma'am.'

'I think it's all so romantic.'

Then Mrs Race put her shovel in. 'Ah,' says she, in that low purring voice, 'but do the men carry guns?'

'Well, yes, ma'am. Some carry guns.'

'Where's your gun, Mr Fynn? I can't see it. Do you possess a gun?'

'Yes, ma'am, I do.'

'Can you use it?'

'That's not for me to say.'

'So modest! I should imagine you could use your gun,' drawls Mrs Race.

'You mean,' says Mrs Thomas, 'that you've actually got the gun and the belt and everything? Did you bring it to Chicago?'

'A gun ain't something a man can leave behind, ma'am.'

'Well said!' murmurs Mrs Race, and tapped her fan on her other hand.

'It's really most exciting,' says Mrs Thomas. 'You mean you've got a gun *here*?'

'Packed away.'

'Well,' sighs Mrs Race, 'maybe it could be unpacked.'

'Oh, would you?' says Mrs Thomas. 'Do you think we could prevail upon you to go put it on? Just for a few minutes. It would be such a thrill to see you wearing your gun and all. Like a legend come to life.'

'Where do you hang it, Mr Fynn?' says Mrs Race, and looked at me, cool and insolent. 'Here somewhere?' and she tapped me on the thigh with that blamed fan of hers.

'Do you think we might induce you to –' says Mrs Thomas. 'It would be such fun!'

'Yes,' says Mrs Race. 'Who knows – you might even draw it for us before the night's out.'

Both of them laughed, but for different reasons.

I stood there and felt my face burning. The night had been a bad one for me. 'All right,' says I, and heard my voice grate. 'If that's what you ladies want, I'll oblige.' Why not? I saw I'd get pleasure out of ranging through all them rich folks, with me heeled, and I figured Mr Quarles would only applaud – the old sharp! With my guns on, I could walk among them knowing that for once I had the advantage.

'Now you're talking,' says Mrs Race. She was more common than a crib-girl in her high-toned way. I wondered how much more of it was going on in that glittering room. Everybody was dressed so smart and acted so polite, but underneath I fancied there was a deal of hunching going on, and nodding and hinting, and folks signalling with their eyes, and old hands being laid on bare white shoulders. I thought of that, and then I thought about the match-girl, and the old panhandlers, and the folks asleep on the grating, and disgust rose up in me. On sudden, I felt as savage as a meat-axe.

I put away a couple of quick drinks, and excused myself to the ladies, and went upstairs and got my gun-belt. I strapped it on in a deliberate way, looked at myself in the mirror, and told myself I was a prize fool. Yet I couldn't help it. I could hear Mrs Race's mocking voice go echoing in my ears, and all the other voices – Quarles with his rot about the West and all his talk about burdens and responsibility, even Belle with her sly approaches and her love of money. There didn't seem no other way that I could answer them: I strapped on the only weapons I had. You could say it was a gesture of desperation by a half-drunk saphead, or you could say that fate had given me the final nudge, and done it in the person of two society ladies, one a fool and the other a whore. I waited in my room till I was more calm, and then I went back to the reception with my guns at my hip.

I was surprised to find the drawing-room was empty, but there was a buzz coming from the doors that led into the gallery, and when I ranged over there, I saw all the folks had flocked in and were facing the far end. I stood at the back, leaning against the door, and watched the proceedings. Mr Quarles was on his hind legs and had launched into a speech. I saw Belle beside him, and another sleek-looking feller next to her. There was an easel near to Quarles, a big one, draped over by a white cloth. He was going to unveil his latest acquisition, by the looks, but he had to do some talking first.

'I want you good people to share with me in enjoying this work of art,' says he. 'That, of course, is the major reason you've been asked here tonight – apart from us having the pleasure of your company. It's the work of Mr Lascelles –' he waved, and the sleekish feller took a bow – 'who you all know to be one of the most eminent artists of our day and age. This is a picture that I commissioned. It was executed at my personal request, and it carries a great deal of meaning for me, summing up as it does a lot that I've seen in my life, the stirring times I've encountered. You all know my feeling for the West, and it ain't only because I earned my first dollar out there. I wanted a picture that would sum up for me the spirit of those adventurous men, and in my opinion Mr Lascelles has done it. He is, as you know, a master of the Realist school. No artist in this country has a higher reputation, nor can command higher fees. Now, Mr Lascelles asked me if I could find him a man to model for this picture, which would save him the sweat of travelling to the Frontier personally, and it so happened that I could oblige him. As some of you may know, I have in my employ just such a man, who started life hard on the Frontier, but who now works for me. What I've done is, I've asked the young feller in question to come along tonight, dressed in exactly the clothes he wore for the sittings, and I've done this so that you can judge for yourselves the brilliant accuracy of the likeness that Mr Lascelles has struck off. But first the unveiling. Mr Lascelles. Thank you.'

Everybody clapped as Lascelles twitched away the sheet and there was a full-length picture of a man with a black hat and shirt, and a studded gun-belt, and shiny boots with silver spurs on them. A regular dandy, he was, with one hand riding on his gun butt. Just a little more of Quarles's flapdoodle, thinks I. Then I got a look at the face, and I froze.

I could hear more clapping going on and then Mr Quarles's voice, far distant, introducing the original. On stalked Seth in the same fancy gear, and postured at them in

152

the same way as in the portrait, hand on gun butt and a mighty resolute expression on his pan. You could see he was enjoying it, the dog! He didn't look much different, save that his face was harder round the eyes.

I started to push forward. I'd been waiting a long time to run up against Seth and I weren't going to let the opportunity slide now. I got further up towards the front of the gallery, and I didn't need to push no more. Folks had seen the kind of stare Seth was fixing me with, and they just fell aside until there was a clear space between him and me.

'What's wrong, boys?' came Quarles's wavering voice.

'Who let him in?' says Belle in a hissing whisper. 'They should have been kept apart.'

'But why?' says Quarles. 'They're old friends, ain't they?' I heard this, and I thought to myself: Quarles ain't in on it, but Belle is, and a cold fury ran through me.

'Hello, Seth,' says I.

'You surprised me, Missouri.' He was smiling. 'You come ranging up on me like a ghost.'

'I want a word with you, Seth.'

'Don't lean on me, that's all, pal.'

'How are things?' says I.

'Things are just great.'

'You're working for Mr Quarles, I hear. I can guess the type of work you do. And look at you now. All done up like some kind of fruit. I can't hardly bear the sight of you.'

'That ain't very friendly, Missouri.'

'Now, boys, cut this out!' says Quarles. Nobody paid any attention. Each of us was watching the other.

'I'll tell you one thing,' says Seth. 'The duds may be phoney, but the irons are real, and I ain't forgotten how to use them, neither, so watch your lip.'

'No, but I'll bet you never used them fair and square, have you, Seth?'

'What do you mean?' he yells.

'Do you remember that, you dog?' I held up my hand with the silvery scar on it.

'You was lucky,' says Seth.

'How do you make that out, Seth?'

'You was lucky that I only meant to wing you. I could have blown you through so easy.'

'You tried, Seth. You murdering rat! You're a liar and a cheat and a murderer!'

'Don't call me that,' says he. 'No man calls me that.'

I fancied I could hear folks breathing. I could glimpse some of them, too, out of the tail of my eye, huddled by the walls, up against the items of Quarles's museum, the single shots and the war-bonnets and all. They should have found a stand-up row like this interesting, but I don't reckon they did.

'*I* call you that, Seth.'

I was empty as a husk by now, my voice echoed in me like I was in a church, and I could feel the stillness all around. I was afloat on the stillness. My gun hand seemed to have grown bigger and it ached from the strain of waiting. I knew then that we was going in, for sure.

Seth knew it, too. I saw it pass over his face. He weren't going to back down, he was going to stand. I saw it in the way he changed his position, straddling his legs a little.

'I'll give you what you never gave,' says I. 'Not if you could help it: I'll give you a true show, all fair and square. I'm calling you to account, Seth Walsh.'

Seth grinned, standing there before his portrait. 'Like

hell,' he says. 'You pious bastard. You always did hang on me like a preacher.'

'This time I'll preach you into the grave.'

'You know what?' says Seth. 'Everybody could always fool you, Mister Fynn. You never knew the score. You was born a fool and now you're going to die a fool. Too bad! I feel sorry for you, when I think on it.'

'You talk too much,' says I. 'You're all talk, and cheap tricks, and shooting from behind.'

'You're going to wish you hadn't said that, Fynn. You're going to wish you gunned me down just now, when you had the chance, because maybe I ain't so pious as you, but I'm the better man.'

I shook my head. 'I can shade you, Seth,' says I. 'I always could shade you. Now make your play – or else crawfish out, which is what you've got in mind.'

'I'll chop bits off you!' he yells.

'Please!' shouts Belle. 'This ain't needful. How can you be so crazy? Oh, please, Seth, honey. Don't fight with him. Don't let him hurt you.'

So there it was. Now I really saw how matters stood between them.

Then Quarles puts in his shovel. 'This is *my* house,' he yells. 'I *forbid* you to start anything here. I forbid it!' but this time Quarles's money didn't give him any edge. He had been called, too, you might say, and once his reputation was put in question, his power was gone. When you choose to face death, you become extraordinary free. No man can order you around then; no authority is worth a straw. You're completely free – though it don't last long, one way or another.

We stood there, with Seth glowering at me, and in the end

155

he went for his gun. I shaded him, like I knew I would, but my aim weren't true. The bullet grazed his head and carried off part of his ear. Blood leapt out and Seth gave a maddened squawk, but meantime, his first shot had hit me in the shoulder and spun me around, which I guess is why he missed with his second attempt. I didn't give him no third opportunity but planted a slug high in his chest that knocked him clean off his feet. The crowd gave a general groan at that. There he was, grovelling on the floor, and there above him was his picture, splashed with his blood. I looked at him, and I didn't want to do no more to him. My gunhand felt heavy, and I remembered Mr Johnston all that time ago, back in Cheyenne, how he put away his weapon after killing the little feller, like he could hardly abide the weight of it. Mine felt like that now.

Seth had struggled back on to his knees. He was holding his gun in both hands now, to steady it. His mouth was full of blood, and his eyes was glazing over. 'Leave it, Seth,' says I. 'Don't force me.'

He was swaying around on his knees. 'Damn you!' he groans. 'You've smashed me all to pieces and I can't get my aim.'

'Call quits,' says I. 'Take your life.'

He gave me a crooked grin, with the blood spilling from his mouth. Seth might have been a treacherous man but he had his share of sand. 'Listen, Fynn,' says he. 'Listen good. I *was* in with Plumer. Yeah, and I plugged that crazy Mr Johnston. You knew nothing!' He was choking and spluttering as he tried to go on. 'I had it over you, Missouri Fynn. Always did. Had your women.' He rolled a clouding brown eye towards Belle. 'Had her, while you was mooning round after her. Always won out ... And now ...' He jerked up his gun and tried to get in a quick shot while my attention was straying for a moment on to thoughts of Belle. It didn't work. I saw his game and, the same instant, I hit him in the head, and that finished him. It was a mercy, really, for he was blown to hell and would never have lasted. I figure it was that final wild slug of Seth's that winged Mr Quarles and brought him down to wallow in the same pool of blood. Master and hired gun, they lay together, with that fool picture staring down at them.

I was still there when the police came. I was feeling beat-out and dreary and unlike running. Anyhow, it was a true show I gave Seth, and I set it up fair and square. What else could I have done more than that?

13

It is right that Fynn should die, not only in the name of justice, but in defence of the fundamental values of our new American civilization.

What I Still Think

I tried to explain my position to the judge at the trial but he just couldn't see it. I told him it was a difference between Seth and me that had to be settled, as a matter of common justice, and he says, if that was so, it should have been brought before the courts. I ask you, what would have been the use of that? Seth and Quarles would have smothered the case, hid it under a heap of money and lies. 'A man has to act according to his lights,' says I. 'Not when it means committing murder,' says the judge. 'It depends what you mean by "murder",' says I. 'Because there's times when a man has to act, and nobody else can do it for him. Besides,' says I, 'Seth got a fair show.' The judge says there ain't no such thing as a fair show, and that I was a disgrace to civilized society, and all decent men would hate my behaviour. He says I was a symptom of the most dangerous and sinister kind. He even dragged Anarchists into it.

I gave up trying to argue. I was making no headway at all. We had different points of view, me and the judge, that much was plain. The other difference between us was, he could hang me in support of his opinion, and that's what he aims to do if my appeal gets turned down. I was talked into

Published by Collins Dove
A Division of HarperCollins*Publishers* (Australia) Pty Ltd
22-24 Joseph Street
North Blackburn, Victoria 3130

First published 1991

Designed by William Hung
Cover design by William Hung
Illustrations by Sarah Wilkins
Typeset by Collins Dove Desktop
Printed in Australia by Griffin Press Pty Ltd.

The National Library of Australia
Cataloguing-in-Publication Data:

Orloff-Falk, Judy.
Choices for success : your happiness in your own hands.

ISBN 0 85924 932 8

1. Success. 2. Self-realization (Psychology). I. Doubleday, Peg.
II. Cloud-Guest, Alexa. III. Title.

that appeal by my lawyer, but I ain't sure I want to go through with it. I think I'd rather be strung up than spend year after year in a little room with bars on the window. That brand of mercy don't appeal to me; I'd rather they was merciless; it would be kinder, in my opinion. Anyhow, I don't have to worry, because I'm pretty sure the appeal is going to be turned down.

They got awful nice to me in jail once they knew they were going to kill me. They give me plenty of grub and let me see the newspapers, and that's how I came across the editorial in the *Mirror*. When I read that high-flown piece, I just knew I had to tell the story as it really was. You have to speak up sometimes, even if nobody's going to hear.

The first paper they brought to the cell was to let me make a declaration about the disposal of my possessions, and I wrote: 'I leave my shirt to Belle Quarles, and my boots to her husband, George Quarles, provided he pulls round.' It was the sight of that first piece of paper that gave me the idea. I asked for more, and the governor says that in the circumstances he was willing to oblige. They brought me in a great sheaf of the stuff, and pens, and ink, and all. That's how I come to write the true story of the bloody affray at Riverside Drive.

If anybody reads it and can still go on preaching and moralizing like the editor of the *Mirror*, well, that's their affair. I shan't be disappointed because I don't reckon I shall ever get to know. Otherwise I might be. I know what I still think.